A BROOKHAVEN PARANORMAL COZY MYSTERY
BOOK 3

HIGH FIDELITY

S.E. BIGLOW

1

Autumn had been a blink-and-you'll-miss-it time in Brookhaven as October rolled into November. Leaves had turned delightful shades of yellows, reds, and oranges. The air had taken on a crispness I'd never gotten back home in London. Having never experienced such a stark change in seasons, I wasn't prepared for the way my magic reacted. Admittedly, figuring out the intricacies of my magic wasn't on my radar when moving to town.

Happily, my powers continued to flourish even as the temperatures dropped. The plethora of plants situated throughout Tania's Bed and Breakfast, which I now called home, flowered under my touch. Plus, High Time's marijuana crop production had tripled thanks to my magic. But the world outside was fading and I felt the sense of impending chill deep in my core. I still wasn't used to waking up to a fogged-over window or the occasional thin sheet of ice on the windshield of Tania's VW Bug. After Brookhaven's first real frost, she'd insisted I use it for my commute. I appreciated the generosity. Although the walk from the B&B to High Time wasn't long, my start time often meant being up before sunrise.

Laying hands on the fallen foliage didn't bring with it a sadness or mourning at the loss of nature's beauty. Instead, I could feel the promise of new life just waiting to take root and bloom again. Even when the last leaves littered the sidewalks of our tiny town, I could see the potential of what would replace the barren leaves in a few short months. Carrying that beauty in the back of my mind dispelled the chill.

The autumn sights and smells weren't the only thing in the air these days. Gerry Webster's son was set to be married in just a couple days. It was all anyone could talk about, especially at Ginny's, the local coffee shop.

I stood by the counter waiting for my to-go order when Ginny appeared carrying several trays of pre-packaged pastries. When I'd first come to town, I pegged her as the town gossip. I'd witnessed her draw information out of the people around her and pass it on in an obnoxious fashion to whoever would listen. In reality, she was a witch like me. But where my powers centered on plants, hers was rooted in the truth.

Ginny and I hadn't gotten off on the best of terms when I moved to town a few months ago. That probably had something to do with the fact that I was an unknown entity with magic of my own. Yet after helping to solve not one but two murders, she'd decided I wasn't so bad to have around. And I had to admit, the coffee she served at her café was the best I'd tasted since leaving England behind. However, winning over Ginny had not improved my social standing with her brother, Chief of Police, Rick Hayes. Thankfully I hadn't had a reason to run afoul of him in recent weeks.

Out of the corner of my eye, I spotted Gerry seated in his usual booth, newspaper laid out on the table in front of him. He looked up and our gazes met. In seconds he was on his feet, sauntering over to me.

"Oh, good, I'm glad I caught you," he said.

"Something I can help you with?"

"I just wanted to be sure that you knew you were invited tomorrow for the wedding. I hadn't gotten your RSVP."

"Oh, that's nice, but I don't even know your son." Come to think of it, I didn't know Gerry well either.

Besides, I couldn't even recall receiving an invitation.

"He's invited the whole town," Ginny piped up. "And an RSVP of no isn't acceptable."

"Ginny's right, we've invited everyone in town and it would really make for a wonderful day to have everyone there."

"Well, thank you for the invitation. I'd be happy to attend," I replied.

"And bring a date," Gerry said, as his phone buzzed, pulling him away from the conversation.

"You want help getting these back to Tania's?" Ginny asked, leaning on the counter opposite me.

"Oh, I was just waiting for a coffee to go," I told her.

Ginny's brown eyes narrowed. "She told me you'd be picking up the desserts for the rehearsal dinner tonight."

What? Had I missed something?

I reached for my own phone just as Tania's number flashed on the screen with an incoming call. "Hi Tania. Everything okay?"

"I am so sorry, Darcy, with everything going on today, I forgot to ask if you'd mind picking up desserts from Ginny's on your lunch break."

I smiled. "It's all right. I'm happy to pick them up."

There was silence on the line for a moment before Tania let out a frustrated sigh. "The caterer just let me know both of her staff called out sick. She's down two servers for tonight."

Tania had agreed to host the bridal party and their out-of-town guests at Gerry's request. I'd been the one to plant the seed in his mind. Before my tenancy at the B&B, Tania's business had struggled to stay afloat. Getting the wedding party booked even just for a few nights was the least I could do to support the woman who'd taken me in and helped me learn to control my magic.

Despite Tania playing hostess for the next two days, the bride had insisted that her caterer do the rehearsal dinner at the B&B. Tania was gracious enough in allowing a complete stranger to use her kitchen, but I knew it bothered her. Tania was an excellent cook.

"I get off work at four. I could be back by four fifteen to help you set up. And if it's really a problem, I could help serve tonight."

"Oh, Darcy, *gracias*. You are a life saver."

"I'll be by in a few with the desserts," I said and ended the call. To Ginny, who still stood across the counter from me, I announced, "I think I'll take that help if you don't mind."

"It's why I offered," Ginny replied with an air of annoyance.

She stashed my to-go cup of coffee amongst some of the bags before scooping up half of them into her arms. Together, we walked to the B&B.

"So, I've heard the rumors that Gerry's son has been married a few times. Do you know what happened?" I broached before we reached the B&B's front porch.

"I know you think I'm a gossip," Ginny began. "But everyone knows he's been married at least three times. I don't know any details other than I know he married the first one when he was young and none of them are dead."

Tania's appearance at the front door cut off any other conversation. She ushered us both into the house, through the foyer, and into the kitchen.

"I'll see you this afternoon," I called to Tania before heading back to High Time to finish my shift, Ginny hot on my heels.

I sprinted home after my shift to find Tania fussing with the linens in one of the rooms.

"You know they aren't going to mind if the linens are perfectly pressed or not," I reminded Tania two hours before the rehearsal dinner. Out-of-town guests and the wedding party weren't due to arrive for another hour at least.

"I will know and my mother raised me to put my best foot forward with guests," she huffed and went back to ironing the bedsheets for the room set aside for the bridesmaids.

"Especially paying guests," Sam called in a sing-song tone as he materialized partway through the closed bedroom door.

Sam was the B&B's resident ghost. He wasn't bound to the property and more often than not could be found down by the boardwalk at sunrise and sunset. He reveled in being sassy, but he was very protective of the B&B and of Tania.

"You better be on your best behavior," Tania chided the ghost as she gestured for me to pass one of the pale blue pillowcases sitting on the bed beside me.

"What? Me? You wound me," Sam said, feigning offense as his incorporeal form passed through the door and into the room.

"No spying on the guests," I reminded him.

He batted his eyelashes—they were jeweled today—at me. "I thought you liked it when I nosed in on their business. I seem to recall you specifically telling me to do that, not two months ago?"

He wasn't wrong. I had asked him to keep an eye on the passengers of a local day cruise who'd been forced to stay at the B&B after one of the other passengers wound up dead. But that had served a purpose since I'd been tracking down a killer.

"I do not approve of just general snooping. It's an invasion of privacy, especially when they can't see you or even know you're here," I replied.

The dark eye makeup Sam sported today turned his translucent complexion ashy as he glared at me. "Thanks for the reminder I'm going to be invisible for the next two days, Darcy," he whined.

"It's not my fault," I retorted.

Well, maybe I bore a little responsibility. I had convinced Gerry to ask Tania if the wedding party could be hosted here. But I hadn't been thinking of Sam when I made the suggestion.

"All right, both of you that's enough," Tania interjected. She set the iron down long enough to check her phone and gave a frustrated sigh. "I suppose you're right and the linens will have to do. Would you mind making up the last bed? The caterer is on her way over and needs help setting up the dinner."

"Happy to help," I replied and watched as she opened the door, leaving it ajar as she disappeared downstairs.

"You're spoiling my fun," Sam noted as I gathered up the freshly ironed bedsheets and carried them down the hall to the room marked 10.

"You heard Tania. You've got to behave yourself," I repeated. "We need to be supportive of Tania. We both know she needs this to go well."

His lips turned into a pout, but he nodded. "Fine, I won't go peeping through doors. But you better mind your manners, too, missy."

"Me? What've I done?" I protested.

"People think our town is quaint and charming, but we don't need the tourists knowing just how supernatural we are. No coaxing the flowers in the dining room to buck up."

I wanted to argue that I didn't do that, but couldn't. I'd grown far more comfortable using my powers around the B&B. Tania had adorned nearly every room on the first floor with something I could practice with—from ornamental grasses to roses.

"I promise, no magic in front of the guests."

"I'm not the only one who is going to be grumpy about the influx of house guests, you know," he noted.

I looked up from stuffing a pillow into its case. I opened my mouth to ask who he was talking about when a dark blue lump on the bed shifted to greens, revealing Beau, the telepathic chameleon I'd befriended since moving to town. If I was being honest, he'd chosen me more than the other way around. His telepathy and ability to camouflage himself and others had come in useful in the last few months. I hadn't stopped to consider what all these other minds would do to Beau.

"I'm so sorry Beau. I didn't realize it would be such a burden for you," I said, sitting beside him and putting a hand on his head.

'Too many thoughts and confusion.'

"What if you stayed at Maggie's until everyone's gone?" I proposed.

I felt Beau's head bob in agreement beneath my fingers. Sam floated just beside the bed. "So, you're at the stage of just leaving telepathic reptiles at each other's apartments now?"

Heat warmed my neck and the tips of my ears. I'd recently admitted that I liked Maggie more than just as a friend and I was fairly certain she felt the same way. But we hadn't even been on a proper date.

But there wasn't anyone else in town I trusted to watch out for Beau than her. She was the town's resident healer and a fellow witch.

"He knows Maggie and it's not like she's got strangers traipsing through her place," I countered.

"Or maybe you need a reason to go ask her to be your plus one to this wedding?" Sam posed.

Gerry's invitation sprang to mind. He'd made certain I knew I had a plus one. Then again, Maggie probably did, too. Still, I'd be lying if I didn't admit asking Maggie had been the first thing I'd considered when he told me. But I hadn't broached the topic.

"Oh, sod off," I said with a laugh and mimed tossing the pillow in Sam's direction.

Setting the pillow aside, I tugged my phone loose from my pocket and hit the third contact on my favorites menu. Maggie's name filled the screen as the line rang. Setting it to speaker, I waited for her to answer.

"Darcy? Is everything okay?" I could hear low murmurs in the background as Maggie answered.

Brilliant one, Darc. She's working.

"Oh, yeah, everything's fine. Well mostly. Apparently Beau isn't a big fan of crowds...so, I was wondering if he might be able to stay at your place for the next few days until the wedding's done?"

I caught the sound of an exhale that bubbled into a laugh. "Sure thing. You can drop him by whenever you want."

"Tania's roped me into helping serve the rehearsal dinner. One of the catering staff bailed. So, I'd need to come meet you now."

"I'm pretty swamped. Everyone's decided to come by for their flu shots."

"I could just bring him by the clinic then," I offered, turning my back to Sam who was making lewd gestures at me.

"Yeah, that should be fine. See you in a bit."

AFTER TANIA ASSURED ME SHE WOULD BE FINE WHILE I settled Beau elsewhere for the next few nights, I donned my coat and headed out into the crisp November air. Wind whipped at my face, biting at my exposed skin, but it didn't numb me like it had when the temperature first dropped. As we made the short trek to the clinic, I let my magic bubble to the surface, feeding the last vestiges of greenery that sprouted through cracks in the sidewalk or trees whose last leaves had not quite fallen. Their color brightened just a little as I stopped and pressed a finger to the ones still clinging to the branches.

By the time Beau and I reached the clinic, the sun was low in the sky and the wind had died down. A long line of people stood in front of the building, clogging up the sidewalk. An older woman with a fluffy black hat and stylish tortoise-shell glasses glared and stuck out her cane to bar me entrance.

"Sorry, I'm not trying to the cut the queue. Just need to get in for something else," I explained, offering up what I hoped was a plaintive and innocent expression.

After a moment, the woman relented and allowed me to sneak past her into the clinic. The familiar surroundings were chaotic as the wails of unhappy children filled the air. Maybe this wasn't the best place to leave Beau after all.

I spotted Maggie coming out from the main exam room. Her short hair looked mussed and her face was flushed, but she smiled when she saw me. She waved me over.

"Let's just get him settled in the back, away from the noise," she said, leading me to the back office.

Beau, who had until this moment been perched invisibly on my shoulder appeared and sauntered down my arm to curl up on the desk. He blinked one eye at me before blending in with the wooden surface beneath him.

"Thanks again for this. I know it's last minute," I said, working to muster the courage to ask her about the wedding invitation.

"How could I say no to that face?" she replied and heat flared up my neck until I realized she meant the dozing reptile beside her.

"So, speaking of last minute requests, Gerry

insisted I attend the wedding along with everyone else in town. Anyway, he's given me a plus one and I don't want to be that person who shows up without at least one other person to talk to," I rambled.

"I'd love to be your plus one," Maggie said with a smile.

"Brilliant. I guess I'll see you in the morning then. We can meet at the B&B and go over together."

"I'll be there with bells on."

Before I could say anything else, the door to the office slammed open and the pharmacist who'd been administering vaccines filled the doorway.

"I need you."

"Duty calls," Maggie said, squeezing my hand before following the young man out into the sea of screaming children and elderly patrons.

I made my way back through the throng and into the evening air with a spring in my step. Asking Maggie to be my plus one had gone even better than I'd hoped. It almost made going to a stranger's wedding worth it. By the time Tania's came into view, the small driveway and surrounding street were filled with cars. I spotted an expensive-looking two-door sports car pulled up onto the lawn with a 'Just Married' bumper sticker. *Rude.*

The moment I stepped into the foyer; I knew taking Beau to Maggie's was the right decision. The cacophony of voices as the wedding party and their guests gathered in the living room was enough to set my teeth on edge. Tania poked her head out of the kitchen.

"Oh good, you're back. Change into something comfortable and help me set out these appetizers."

I took the stairs two at a time to my room, trading my vibrant blue High Time work shirt for a dark blue blouse and my jeans for a pair of charcoal grey slacks. When I returned to the first floor, I found the kitchen buzzing with activity. I took the tray of canapés from Tania and headed to the dining room. I'd spotted a dozen lobster tails and steaks waiting to be prepped on the counters. Gerry had spared no expense. Here's hoping the evening and the nuptials went off without a hitch.

2
____

The B&B thrummed with overlapping conversations and more bodies than I'd ever seen filling the space a little after seven o'clock. I studied the caterer, whose name I'd learned was Clara as she darted from place to place in the kitchen. Tania watched her, too. Though if I had to guess why, she was keeping tabs on the stranger in her kitchen to ensure nothing ended up broken. I could see her trailing behind Clara with a rag, wiping up messes left haphazardly on the countertops.

"Here, take those out," Clara said with a snap of her fingers to get my attention.

She pointed to several baskets of dinner rolls and plates of butter. Tania moved to scoop them up, but I took half the load out of her arms.

"Gracias," she said, her cheeks were flushed from the heat of the oven and the pots on the stove. She might not be the one cooking, but that didn't mean the atmosphere wasn't affecting her.

I followed her into the dining room where Tania had squeezed every available chair around the table. I spotted Gerry huddled in a corner with a somewhat younger man who sported the same prominent nose and high cheekbones. He'd also been introduced as Andrew, the groom. I set the rolls and butter down on the table in what had to be last available square inch of space not already taken up by larger serving dishes.

"I think the bride and the bridesmaids are in the living room. Would you mind letting them know everything is ready?" Tania nudged my shoulder as she started circulating through the guests already lingering around Andrew and Gerry. Where she'd gotten the wine bottle she proffered I couldn't say.

I wound my way through a few older couples who were sitting near the back window overlooking the fenced-in yard and into the living room to find the bride-to-be sporting a bright pink sash. She clutched a wine glass in her hands as she laughed, surrounded by three other women who looked to be in their twenties or early thirties. They each sported a large button with the word, 'Bridesmaid.' They'd been here most of the afternoon and if the several empty wine bottles sitting in the kitchen were any indication, this wasn't her first glass.

"Elise, I'm so sad your mom couldn't make it tonight," the bride-to-be said, her lips turning down in a pout.

The tallest of the three bridesmaids whose hair sported an elegant series of twists culminating in a knot at the nape of her neck gave an exaggerated nod. "I know, Casey, she really wanted to come, but she just couldn't get away from work until the big day tomorrow. But I promise, she's going to be here to walk you down the aisle. And she totally gave me strict instructions to give you as many hugs as possible until she gets here."

To make her point, Elise swooped in and pulled Casey into a tight embrace. The other two brides-maids joined in the embrace and they all devolved into a fit of semi-drunken giggles. From the far side of the room, I caught the soft click of a camera snapping the candid moment. The photographer, whose name I thought was Courtney, had been slipping from room to room since I'd come back from dropping Beau off with Maggie. She was dressed in neutral brown tones that almost made her an afterthought. Then again, I suppose that was the mark of a good wedding photographer. They went around unseen to get the best shots. The only thing that stood out was a vibrant red gem hanging on a cord around her neck. She caught me looking and tucked it beneath her sweater.

"Sorry to interrupt the group hug ladies, but dinner is being served," I said, edging into the conversation, and letting Courtney blend into the background again.

Casey wiggled free of her supportive huddle and looked at me, cheeks flushed. "Dinner already?"

I nodded. "I think we've got a special spot for the wedding party at the head of the table," I said and gestured back toward the dining room.

"Thanks," Casey said, straightening her sash and leading the rest of her entourage from the room.

Elise trailed after the others, stopping to study me. Her dark brown eyes narrowed. "Who are you again?"

"I'm Darcy. I live here at Tania's and I'm attending the wedding tomorrow. The groom's dad invited the whole town. Anyways, I'm just helping out tonight, because one of the servers took ill," I rambled, suddenly uncomfortable in the woman's presence.

"Oh. Right," Elise muttered and left me standing there in the opening that led back to the dining room.

I caught sight of Tania gesturing for me to return

to the kitchen. I darted through the dining room as everyone settled in. I entered the space to find Clara laying the last of the lobster tails onto a tray.

"These are ready if anyone wants seconds," she said, wiping her brow.

I spotted four plates set aside on the counter, which I hoped were meant for us. As awkward as it was having someone else running the kitchen, I couldn't deny the food Clara prepared looked and smelled amazing.

"Feel free to grab a plate," Clara added and loosened the tie keeping her dark hair out of her face. She smoothed it back into a ponytail before bending down to check something through the oven window. As she did so, I noticed a slender necklace with a deep yellow stone slip from beneath her shirt. She stood and tucked the necklace back beneath the fabric.

"We need more wine," Andrew's voice boomed from the dining room just as I reached for a plate.

"Guess I can't eat just yet." I sighed as I picked up the partially open bottle of red wine and a newly opened bottle of white.

I stepped into the dining room and started at the end of the table closest to the kitchen, where one of the groomsmen sat. I held up both bottles of wine and he gestured wordlessly to the red. I'd done a little serving back in London during university, so I knew enough to avoid reaching over him to get to his glass. As I made my way slowly around the table toward the wedding party, I silently took stock of the assembled group. I had been expecting even more guests since Andrew and Casey were coming to Brookhaven from out of town. Yet, there were only ten extra people who'd come in tonight for the festivities.

By the time I made it around the table to where Andrew sat beside Gerry, I'd run out of the red and the bottle of white was half empty. "Hope the white's okay," I told the groom, gesturing for him to pass me his glass.

He glanced my direction, almost surprised I'd even spoken. I picked up on the heavy scent of alcohol on his breath as he leaned over and clamped his hand down on my right arm. "Do I look like I care what you've got?"

"I can get you something else if you'd prefer," I said through pursed lips, trying to tug my arm free.

"Andrew, stop harassing the poor girl," Gerry said, fixing his son with a disapproving glare.

Andrew blinked slowly, looked down at his hand and pulled it away. "Sorry. White's fine."

I hastily poured the remainder of the bottle into his glass. Swallowing the sudden lump in my throat, I croaked out, "Anyone else need a top up?"

The last few people around the table shook their heads. I was about to take my leave when Tania appeared and darted around the other end of the table.

"Sorry to interrupt, but the florist just arrived and is asking for you," Tania informed Elise loud enough for me to catch it.

"Oh no," Casey whined. "What's wrong now?"

"I promise, nothing is going to go wrong with the flowers," Elise said and followed Tania out of the room.

Tania trailed after the maid of honor and I fell in line behind her. We settled ourselves at the kitchen table with the plates of food and I dug in. As much as I felt like a traitor for thinking it, Clara's cooking was excellent. She'd marinated the steak beautifully.

At the far end of the kitchen, I watched Elise speak with a petite woman in a vibrant purple and orange dress. "Colleen, I thought we had everything set at the venue," Elise's voice carried in our direction despite the whir of the fan above the stove going full blast.

"Just wanted to triple check whether you needed me to do anything special with the bride's bouquet."

That seemed an odd thing to ask this late in the preparations. Not that I knew much about weddings, but didn't most people nail down all of those little details long before the eve of the wedding day?

"No, we've got that covered. Just be sure you've set the flowers in the chapel at the altar."

"How's our girl holding up?" Colleen's voice lowered to a whisper.

"She's nervous, but it's all going to go off without a hitch," Elise assured the woman.

"Good. I'll see you in the morning, then." Colleen gave Elise a brief one-armed hug before departing.

I'd been so focused on the conversation; I hadn't noticed Clara slide an extra basket of bread across the counter. "I need to start plating the desserts. Can one of you take this in?"

"I can do that," Elise offered as she walked back through the kitchen.

She sauntered past where Tania and I sat, as if we were invisible.

"Everything's all set," Elise announced to the table, locking eyes with Casey as she set the basket down and retook her seat.

"You really are the best," Casey proclaimed, draping herself over the other woman in a sloppy hug. "I don't know what I'd do without you."

"Careful there, Andrew, you might have some competition," a bearded man at the other end of the table called with a laugh.

A few other people around the table joined in the laughter. I peered through the opening between the kitchen and the dining room in time to see Andrew's cheeks brighten in what I assumed was embarrassment. Casey unwound herself from Elise and sat up. Andrew opened his mouth to speak, but changed his mind.

"Don't worry, son, it's clear she only has eyes for you." Gerry's voice carried.

"Remind us how you two met," one of the guests, an older woman, interjected.

"At a charity event at my alma mater. Casey was running the event and I was donating. I knew right then that she was something special."

"That's sweet."

"Convincing her to go on a date with me took far longer than I would have thought," he added. "Anyway, I won her over in the end and she's going to make me the luckiest man on the planet tomorrow," Andrew boasted.

The conversation died down in the other room and I turned my attention back to the food in front of me. "Can I ask you something?" I directed my question to Tania.

"Of course."

"I get the sense Gerry and his family are kind of an institution in town. Like Rick and Ginny. What's the story there?"

"Well, Gerry and I grew up together. He has a brilliant mind and invested in green energy long before a lot of people. He made a name for himself, along with a lot of money and retired early. Andrew went to private school from what I remember. So, this isn't really his home, not like it is Gerry's."

"Gerry mentioned there'd been other marriages and so did Ginny."

"He allegedly left some broken hearts in his wake. I think Gerry sees it as a point of disappointment, although he doesn't say much. I think that's why he's so intent on making this last one as memorable as possible."

"Well, I think it's time we head out," a deep male voice announced to the relative silence of the dinner guests.

His announcement was enough to draw my attention. He was already on his feet and waving for Andrew to follow him. A redheaded man with a buzz cut stood as well. Andrew eyed them both with a wary expression.

"Benny, Marco, I thought I'd told you both no bachelor party."

Benny, the redhead, shrugged. "Best man prerogative. Your blushing bride had her chance to celebrate and we wouldn't be doing our groomsmen duties if we didn't do the same." He turned to Casey. "Now, don't worry, we'll have him back in time for the ceremony."

"And in one piece," Marco added.

Andrew appeared to mull the decision over for a moment before he threw his hands up in the air. "All right. But we better be going somewhere good."

Benny clapped him on the shoulder. "Just you wait."

The three men along with one or two of the other male guests left the dining room just as Tania entered the room with the desserts I'd brought home earlier from Ginny's.

The soft click of Courtney's camera caught my attention as she continued to circulate around the room, capturing the moments between smaller groups of people. As Tania came back with the tray of half-empty dessert plates, I asked, "Did she get something to eat?"

"No. Poor thing hasn't stopped working since she got here," Tania answered.

There was still plenty of food left to make up a decent plate. Courtney slipped from the dining room again back into the living room. I excused myself from the kitchen and followed her.

"You should get something to eat." My words startled her and she nearly dropped her camera. "Sorry, didn't mean to sneak up on you."

"I'm just so used to people not noticing I'm here," she murmured.

"I could go make you a plate if you'd like," I offered.

"I'm okay, thanks."

I pointed to the camera. "Get any good shots?"

"You don't have to make small talk. You can go back to whatever you were doing."

"Honestly, I was just doing a favor for a friend. I think everyone's taken care of for now anyway. Please, I'd love to see your work."

Courtney looked down at the camera before waving me over and turning it so I could see the screen. She flicked through candid shots of guests in mid-conversation, often smiling and laughing. There were mostly photos of Casey and her bridesmaids, very few of Andrew.

"Andrew must not be very photogenic," I observed.

"He insisted we wait to get more photos of him at the wedding itself," she said, but flipped through a few others to show a couple of shots where Andrew was visible. "But I snuck a few when he wasn't looking."

"It must be an interesting profession, capturing people's happiness for posterity. Getting to share in that joy."

"Spoken like someone whose never been married," Courtney replied. "Sorry, you know I think maybe I should take that plate. I get grumpy when I'm hungry."

"Lobster, steak or both?" I said with a smile.

"Both."

I walked back into the kitchen to find Tania was already putting together a plate. I arched a brow in confusion, but she mouthed 'Sam' and handed it to me. Our resident ghost was trying to find ways to still be seen in a house of mundane guests. At least he was mostly behaving himself.

I carried the plate to Courtney. She settled in one of the chairs in the living room and dug into the food. I turned to rejoin Tania when I found Elise standing there. "Casey is going to call it an early night. We have hair and makeup at ten tomorrow and then we have to get to the church by eleven," she said, addressing Courtney.

"I'll be there for before shots."

"Thanks," Elise said and retreated to the dining

room just long enough to escort a tipsy Casey upstairs to her room.

In short order, the rest of the guests retired to their rooms. If all went well, wedding bells would be ringing by noon.

3

———

The atmosphere in the B&B on the morning of the wedding was charged. *Literally.* I gave myself an electric shock the moment I reached for the bathroom door. I winced and sucked the tip of my finger where the shock had zapped me. I could hear muffled voices from within.

"Case, it's okay," one of the bridesmaids said in a coaxing tone.

"I checked his room, he wasn't there. The bed wasn't even slept in." Casey's words ended in a sob.

"They probably just stayed out late and crashed somewhere else. I mean, Andrew's dad lives in town, right?"

Casey gave another sob and loud sniffle. I tried to back away, but my weight shifted enough on the floorboards to betray my presence. The conversation stopped within the bathroom. The door squeaked open and swung inward to reveal Casey with curlers in her hair and red rims under her eyes.

"Sorry, didn't mean to eavesdrop." I tried to give her a sympathetic look. "I think your friend's right. He's probably just had a late night at his stag party and gone to sleep it off somewhere."

Casey mouthed the words 'stag party' in confusion. Her friend appeared at her side and wrapped the bride in a shawl. "Come on. We need to get you cleaned up, so you're ready for hair and makeup. Everything is going to be fine."

I waited for them to pass by before I walked in and set about getting myself ready. When I stepped out of the shower a few minutes later, I half-expected to be greeted by Sam. Despite him being Tania's eyes and ears the night before, he'd taken the directive to lay low seriously. I had to admit I was a little disappointed. I had expected him to offer a full commentary on his thoughts of the wedding party and guests.

I wiped the fog off the mirror and winced as I caught sight of a fresh bruise on my right forearm, an inch above my wrist. The image of Andrew grabbing my arm the night before flashed in my mind.

Had he really grabbed me hard enough to leave a mark? Surely the bruise was just an accident. I tugged my sleeve down to cover it.

As I headed for the stairs, I caught Casey's voice from down the hall, asking if someone thought makeup would cover the redness under her eyes. At least she didn't seem to be crying anymore. I reached the first floor just as Tania appeared with an apron tied tight around her waist.

"I thought you confirmed that Clara is catering brunch for the wedding party at the venue," I noted, gesturing to the apron.

"I was cleaning," she answered and undid the apron strings from her waist.

I followed her into the kitchen to find the counters back to their pristine condition. Yet another reason I had to believe she possessed more than just empathic abilities.

"I hope Casey has calmed down," Tania noted softly as she joined me, reaching one hand toward the coffee pot.

"You heard her, too?"

"Poor thing was up at five o'clock this morning pacing the front hall."

"He's got a mobile phone, doesn't he? Why doesn't she just call him and put her mind at ease?"

"Sometimes stress makes people forget the logical option," Tania answered. "And weddings are nothing if not stressful."

Before I could comment further, a sharp knock at the front door cut the conversation short. Tania's hands were still busy with the coffee pot and I left the brightness of the kitchen for the more muted lighting of the front hall. The knock came a second time as I reached the door.

"Coming," I called and opened the door.

A slender woman with wisps of grey at her temples stood on the threshold. She wore a full winter coat complete with faux red fur trim at the neck and wrists. I spotted the travel case beside her.

"Are you going to just stand there or can I come in?" she demanded.

I gawked at her in stunned silence for a moment. The woman acted like I ought to have some idea of who she was. "Um, are you here for the wedding?"

She let out an exasperated huff. "Of course, I am."

"Mom," Elise's voice floated down the stairs behind me and I turned to see the maid of honor standing halfway down the staircase, her hair done up in curlers. "I was worried you weren't going to make it."

"Sorry, here let me get that for you," I offered and reached for the woman's suitcase.

"I can carry my own luggage thank you."

I took a step back to allow her entry into the house and she immediately ascended the stairs to meet her daughter, Elise where she stood.

"Casey has been a mess all morning. Panicking she would have no one to walk her down the aisle," Elise explained while she embraced her mother. Without another word, they disappeared from view. I could hear an exclamation of, "Thank God you're here," from Casey before the telltale sound of doors slamming reverberated in the space.

"Okay then," I muttered and retreated to the kitchen. Tania closed the oven, setting a tray of fresh muffins on the counter to cool.

"You baked," I said, eyeing the pastries.

"Let's just say after last night, I needed a little stress relief." She pointed to a cup of coffee on the opposite counter. "And something tells me we're both going to need the fortification."

She wasn't wrong. I greedily took a long sip from the mug and eyed a muffin from across the room. "So, what's exactly the plan for today?"

"I assume the bridal party will meet over at the church for their brunch. Then the ceremony starts at noon I believe."

"I should go over and meet Maggie before then," I said.

I caught the smile on Tania's lips. "You sound happy when you talk about her, you know."

"It's not like it's a date or anything," I denied weakly.

Tania just chuckled to herself. "But you want it to be."

I couldn't even argue with her. Not when she could literally sense my emotions. So, I settled for snatching a muffin and carrying my food into the dining room. To my surprise, Gerry sat there. He was reading the paper and that part didn't surprise me one bit. When we'd first met a few months ago, he'd just come back to town after being away for a while. He'd informed me he was reading every paper that had been put out in his absence. He must have spent all day reading, because he'd caught up far quicker than I'd have assumed.

"Morning," I greeted and set my coffee down beside him.

"Oh, morning," he said, setting the paper down. I could see the beginnings of dark circles under his eyes.

"You excited for the big day?" I prodded.

"I'm not the one walking down the aisle. But will admit I'll be glad when the vows have been exchanged and they're off on their honeymoon. It's been a lot on my plate."

He was the one paying for the whole affair. "It did seem a bit unfair to heap the whole thing on you."

"Oh, I was happy to do it. Casey is a sweet girl. Both of her parents are no longer with us, I'm afraid."

"I hadn't realized that."

"The maid of honor's mother will be giving her away."

"I've met her. She's a bit intense."

Gerry laughed. "Can't say I've actually had the pleasure."

I pointed to the ceiling. "She just got in and went up with the girls. Casey sounded relieved she made it."

He nodded, lapsing into silence. His fingers picked at the edges of the newspaper on the table in front of him.

I took another sip of coffee. "Not that I'm prying, but if it's not the money part of it, then why are you so focused on them getting to their honeymoon?"

"If I'm being honest, I'm a little doubtful this is going to work out. It's just that she's so much younger than Andrew."

"You worry she's taking advantage of him?'

"Oh, no. She's too decent of a person to be after his money. I just worry she's not really aware of what she's getting into with Andrew."

"What do you mean?"

Gerry opened his mouth to speak, but shut it and shook his head. "Nothing. Forget I mentioned it. I should go see where he and the rest of his entourage ended up last night. She'd kill him if he was late to his own wedding."

With that, Gerry folded his paper, tucked it neatly beneath his left arm, and exited the dining room. I sat there in confusion, coffee going cold in the mug before me.

I tried to shake off the feeling of unease that settled over me as I finished breakfast. Maybe Gerry was just having father of the groom nerves. Were those a thing? I was beginning to regret sending Beau to stay at Maggie's for the duration of the wedding festivities. He could have explained what Gerry wasn't willing to say.

Speaking of Maggie, I needed to get ready to meet her. We had a wedding to attend.

I wasn't used to dressing up so fancy. I hadn't worn heels in ages and my feet ached even before I'd slipped them on. I made it down to the first floor of the bed and breakfast before kicking them off and changing into flats. I'd tamed my hair into a top knot and pulled a light jacket on over my dress before making the short walk to Maggie's place. We'd initially agreed to meet at the church, but it felt more appropriate for me to pick her up for such an occasion.

"You look great," she complimented, meeting outside before I even had a chance to ring the bell. She'd been expecting me.

"Thanks." I took a moment to assess her ensemble. She wore an emerald green dress and black sweater that accentuated all the right curves. My heart hammered a little faster in my chest. "You look brilliant, too."

"We should get going. Don't want to miss the good stuff."

Maggie looped her arm through my left one and led the way toward the heart of town. We passed Ginny's which was closed with a sign reading 'Back for Dinner.' That felt a little odd to me. In the few months I'd lived here, I'd never seen Ginny's closed. But if Gerry had insisted everyone in town come, it made sense.

"I still can't believe Gerry invited the whole town," I said.

"He's got pull when he wants to," Maggie replied.

"You were already planning to go, weren't you?" I sighed.

"Maybe I wanted to be asked by a beautiful woman to be her date."

My mouth went dry. She thought this was a date. *Don't panic, Darcy.* I wanted this to be a date, too. "You want this to be a date?"

"Only if you want it to be one."

"I'd like that," I admitted before I could stop myself.

"Then that's settled." She gave me a broad grin and tugged me along toward the church.

It was a short walk, like most places in Brookhaven, to our destination. I wasn't much for religion and hadn't ever ventured inside. The building was pristine white with a bell tower and wide clock that perpetually seemed frozen at 8:30. No wonder it never chimed on the hour.

The front doors were open even though the air had turned chilly as guests filtered in. I saw immediately why Gerry had sought to invite the whole town. The side designated for the bride was woefully unattended, save for some people about my age clustered toward the front of the chapel. I spotted Ginny in a bright blue dress directing people to seats.

Our gazes met as we reached where Ginny stood. She silently took in Maggie's and my linked arms. She tilted her head to one side for a moment before giving what I assumed was an approving nod.

"I know you're here for the groom side, but we've run out of space," Ginny announced and pointed to the right side of the chapel. "Find a seat over there."

"Thanks." I led Maggie inside and we slid into a pew near the back. I could see Courtney moving around the periphery of the room, snapping shots of the floral arrangements up by the altar. I also saw Colleen, the florist. From this distance, the petite woman with almost blonde white hair looked even more diminutive. Still, as she turned I thought I caught the sparkle of something green around her neck. Andrew and his groomsmen were nowhere to be seen and I checked the time. The wedding was meant to start in ten minutes.

"Are you okay?" Maggie's voice was soft in my ear.

"What? Oh, yeah. Why?"

"You're fidgeting. And you've checked the time twice in the last thirty seconds."

"I guess I'm just anxious for things to get started. I'm honestly not that much for weddings. And if I'm being honest, the whole morning's been a bit off. Andrew and his mates didn't come back beforehand. Maybe Casey was right to worry."

I set my phone down and absently slid my sweater sleeve up toward my elbow, exposing the bruise.

"What's that?" she demanded, reaching for my arm to examine it.

"It's nothing," I said, wincing in spite of my words when she prodded it with the tip of her index finger.

"Darcy, tell me what happened."

"He didn't mean to, but he'd had a few drinks last night. He was trying to get my attention and just grabbed me."

"Who?" Her tone was low.

"Andrew."

Maggie's lips turned into a scowl. Her gaze went unfocused for a moment as her brow knit together in thought.

"I'll be right back," she announced and moved to get past me.

"Where are you going?" I called after her. "Please don't make a big thing out of this."

"Bathroom." She didn't even look over her shoulder as she fought the incoming current of guests and disappeared from view.

I wasn't sure what to make of her hasty retreat. I turned my attention to the people around me. I spotted some familiar faces among the crowd, including Chief Hayes and Vinnie, both seated across from me. Vinnie offered me a discreet wave, which I returned. Up near the altar, Colleen stepped aside to speak with Courtney. Courtney snapped a few photos before checking something in her hand —maybe her phone—and hurrying toward the back of the church. Colleen headed for a side door behind the altar.

I checked the time again. It was already fifteen minutes past noon and Andrew and the groomsmen were still missing. The priest shifted his weight from foot to foot in front of the altar, clearly growing impatient.

"Where's Andrew and the groomsmen?" someone a couple rows ahead of me asked, their voice carrying thanks to the high ceilings designed to project sound.

A very good question.

The other attendees started shifting in their seats. Some cast backward glances down the aisle, maybe hoping to see whether the bridal party had appeared. Except for Maggie, Courtney, and Colleen, I hadn't seen anyone else come or go in the last few minutes. Across the aisle, Chief Hayes leaned over and whispered something in Vinnie's ear. He glanced up at the altar and back to him before shrugging.

I resisted the urge to check my phone for another five minutes. After confirming Maggie had left with her phone, I texted her.

'Everything okay?'

No response.

Where was Maggie? Surely she wasn't still in the loo. Maybe I ought to go check on her. As I stood to leave the chapel, a sense of dread washed over me. Something definitely wasn't right. The doors leading outside of the church sat closed and Ginny had gone to sit with her brother. I wasn't sure which way Maggie had gone. I spotted Courtney standing a few paces away.

I tapped her on the shoulder to catch her attention. "Sorry to bother you, but could you point me to the ladies' room?"

She gestured down a nearby flight of stairs without speaking, phone pressed to her ear. I descended the stairs, moving out of range to overhear her call. My stomach tightened with every step. I reached the bottom and stopped as my heart hammered against my ribs.

"Maggie?" My voice came out in a raspy whisper.

"In here!" Her voice rang out like a bell and I hurried forward.

I turned into the bathroom to find Andrew sprawled face down on the floor. Maggie sat beside him; her hands pressed against the back of his neck where several loops of something cinched tight around his throat.

4

———

The world shifted off its axis and I staggered sideways against the bathroom door. My vision grayed out as my mind fought to process what I was seeing in front of me. *This can't be happening again.* Couldn't I go just a few months without having to deal with another dead body?

Maybe he's not dead?

"Is he ...?" I forced out the words as the world came back to me, doing my best to focus on Maggie and not Andrew's prone form.

"I can't get a pulse," she answered in a strained tone.

Part of me wanted to unwind the cords from Andrew's throat. Surely that would help him breathe again. But that would mean touching the man and I knew enough not to contaminate the scene.

"What happened?" I knelt beside Maggie, noting the way her hands shook. "You looked pretty upset when you saw the bruise on my arm."

Maggie's gaze drifted to my arm. "Could you blame me?"

I couldn't. But it also seemed like something that might be of interest to a certain police chief sitting in the chapel upstairs. "No, I couldn't. I'm honestly kind of flattered you care about me that much."

"I protect the people I care about." Her voice grew stronger as she spoke.

"So, you didn't come to confront him?"

She blinked rapidly a few more times "No. Though I heard someone say they were getting ready in the fellowship hall on the other side of basement."

"Then why'd you come here?"

"I heard this voice in my head, a warning that Andrew was in trouble."

"Beau?"

"I don't' know. Could have been. He's never really communicated with me. Not even after that lunatic boat captain. But it was almost like a compulsion." She shook her head as if to clear the cobwebs from her mind.

She uncurled her hands to reveal angry rend indentations that looked frightfully similar to the width of the cord wrapped around Andrew's neck. And there were smears of blood on her fingertips.

"How'd your hands get like that?" I prodded.

She looked down and her brow creased. "I ... I think I was tugging to try and loosen them."

"And the blood?"

"I don't know."

"Did you see anyone on your way down here?" I recalled seeing Courtney standing just beyond the chapel. And she'd been on the phone. But with who? And for how long?

"I was so focused on getting here that it was like I had tunnel vision."

"You didn't call for help." My words came out as an accusation and I hated myself for it.

"I'm a healer, Darcy." When she looked at me the expression on her face was clear. She'd hoped her own magic would have been enough to revive the groom.

"You are an amazing witch, but not even you can raise the dead," I reminded her, giving her hands a squeeze.

"God, I didn't even try," she rasped.

I needed to get Maggie out of the room and away from Andrew's body. A potential crime scene was no place to try to calm her down or help focus her thoughts. I stood and allowed my upward momentum to pull Maggie to her feet. Carefully, we both stepped over Andrew's legs and shuffled back to stand at the bottom of the stairs. In the back of my mind, I noted that no one else had come looking for Andrew or the remainder of the wedding party.

"We need to tell Chief Hayes what's happened," I said, my voice level.

"Never thought I'd hear you wanting to talk to Rick voluntarily," Maggie said.

"Believe me, it's never at the top of my to do list, but my gut tells me Andrew didn't choke himself to death. That makes it police jurisdiction."

"Right." Maggie turned to head upstairs, but paused before she'd made it up the next riser. "There was a smell."

"Come again?'

"When I walked in, there was a smell ... flowery. But I couldn't tell you what it was."

Flowers were in my wheelhouse. Or at least they were in the vicinity and I had to believe that's why she mentioned it. Leaving her on the stairs, I returned to bathroom and inhaled deeply. She was right, there was something there, but I couldn't place it. It wasn't like I had an eidetic memory for floral scents or anything.

Closing my eyes, I focused again, this time with my magic. I turned inward, seeking out the kernel of power that resided deep within me. It sprang to life and filled my mind's eye in an instant. Where once getting hold of my magic had been a battle, it came to me with ease now. It was truly amazing what some support and nurturing could do. The mental manifestation of my power bloomed into a beautiful white lily and I felt my magic fill me from head to toe. My whole body thrummed with energy and when I opened my eyes, everything around me came into sharper relief. I noted the angry red indentations marring Andrew's skin around the cords lashed about his neck.

The flowery scent was stronger now and I tried to commit it to my sense memory for use later. Something metallic hit me as I inched closer to Andrew's feet. I cocked my head to one side and inhaled again.

"What's that coppery smell?" My voice was soft.

My magically enhanced senses picked up on something red marring the edge of the sink in the tiny space. I craned my neck and peered down at Andrew whose head faced the sink. Maybe there was something on his cheek. I longed to turn the man over and see what might be hiding there, but I wasn't going to touch him. As far as I could tell, there wasn't anything around my magic could latch on to in order to lift him.

There wasn't much else I was going to get from the scene. Vague floral scents and hints of blood weren't much to go on anyway. I retreated back to the stairs where Maggie waited. As I let my magic recede from the forefront of my senses, my ears popped and I winced at the discomfort. Maybe my powers had focused on everything too much and this was just my body's way of coming back to equilibrium.

It was time to notify Chief Hayes.

I expected there to be more of a commotion in the chapel since Andrew still hadn't appeared. The groomsmen were also absent, which remained suspicious. They had to know Andrew was missing. Wouldn't one of them have come to find out what was going on?

My stomach did a series of acrobatic flips as I approached the row where Ginny, Chief Hayes, and Vinnie sat. I didn't want to make a scene. At least, not yet.

"Chief," I said loud enough to get his attention.

Chief Hayes looked up at me with those intense brown eyes, always flecked with hints of amber. "Something I can help you with Miss Ingram?"

"I need you and Vinnie to come with us. It's urgent."

I could see Ginny's jaw working, as if she wanted to say something. She remained silent for once and simply slid out of the row to allow her brother and Vinnie to exit.

Despite my attempt to keep this low key, I still felt eyes on me as I led the two men out of the chapel. Maggie brought up the rear.

"What's going on?" Chief Hayes repeated as I started down the stairs.

"It's easier if I show you," I answered.

The space at the bottom of the stairs felt cramped with four people. I wanted to retreat and let the professionals handle the situation. I couldn't make my body obey my desire to leave.

Vinnie stepped forward, bent down over Andrew's body, and pressed a finger to the man's neck. "He's gone," he said, looking up at Chief Hayes.

Chief Hayes' jaw tightened as he clamped down on some no doubt choice words that weren't appropriate for the venue. As the chief pivoted to look at Maggie and I, I caught sight of a small cut on the man's cheek which probably came from the sink. And it explained the origin of the blood on Maggie's fingers. The cords wrapped around his neck were a jumble, but I could see snatches of color; red, yellow, green. I also spotted a pale flower petal pressed firm against Andrew's suit jacket.

"You two are going to tell me what happened,"

Chief Hayes said, pulling my attention.

"Darcy isn't involved," Maggie said, stepping up to physically put herself between me and the police chief.

"I'll be the judge of that."

"We need to notify the bride," Vinnie said, standing to his full height.

Chief Hayes nodded. "They were getting ready upstairs."

Vinnie stood still, as if the idea of making the notification terrified him. I couldn't blame him. It would terrify me, too. Upon closer inspection, the way his lips pressed together and his eyes widened, I realized it wasn't terror. It was embarrassment.

"You want me to do that?" he finally croaked out.

"You have a problem with that?" The chief's tone turned gruff.

"It's just ... well," he stammered.

"I could go with you," I offered before I could think better of the suggestion. I had no reason to be there, except I was a woman and suspected that was Vinnie's hang up.

"You'll still need to give your statement," the chief replied.

"I will. But I think you'll want to talk to Maggie first since she's the one who discovered the body." I stopped short of adding 'this time.'

Chief Hayes' displeasure was evident in the scowl he now wore, but he didn't protest further. I offered Vinnie a quick shoulder pat before taking the lead up to the main floor. Voices filtered out of the chapel as people realized something was off.

"Thanks," Vinnie said softly in my ear as we made our way upstairs to where the bridal party had been preparing.

"I honestly didn't think he'd go for it," I said when we reached the top of the stairs. I could hear muffled voices coming from within the room.

"For what it's worth, I'm sorry you keep getting mixed up in things like this."

"Me too," I replied and gestured for him to announce his presence. The sooner we got this over with the better.

Vinnie's hand shook as he raised it and knocked on the door. The voices inside stopped and the door opened to reveal Casey's face. "What's going on? Why haven't we started yet?"

"Miss, my name is Officer Vinnie Merchant, I need to speak with you in private," Vinnie said.

"You can say whatever it is in front of everyone," Casey said.

"I'm sorry to inform you, but Andrew Webster is dead."

5

Casey's expression melted at his words and a gut-wrenching sob erupted from her mouth. Her body collapsed to the ground amid the elegant folds of her wedding dress as the door swung inward to reveal Elise and the other bridesmaids standing in a tight circle behind the girl, mouths all agape. Elise's mother knelt by Casey's side, wrapping her in a protective maternal embrace.

"You're wrong," Casey howled. Her hands shook as she fought to maintain her makeup, but only succeeded in smearing mascara across her lower lids.

"I am so sorry, but he was discovered in the bathroom in the basement," Vinnie answered, falling into his role as police officer.

He didn't need me anymore, but no one seemed

to notice me. In their world, I was unimportant. I took a step back from the scene to give them some semblance of privacy in this moment of tragedy and horror. No one should have to lose the person they loved, let alone on their wedding day.

"We are going to be strong," Elise's mother told Casey as she eased the young woman to her feet. She guided the bride to a nearby couch and got her settled. Elise and the other two bridesmaids immediately descended on Casey, squeezing in around her to show their support.

"We're going to need to notify everyone else, but also I'm going to need to take everyone's statements," Vinnie explained.

"What for? We've been up here all morning," Casey replied through a sniffle.

"It's just procedure," he said, his tone softening. "I promise, I'll try to be as unobtrusive as I can. Just give me a few minutes to make notifications and I'll be back up."

"I need to see him," Casey exclaimed, struggling to free herself from the arms encircling her on the couch.

"I'm afraid I can't let you do that," Vinnie said. He looked at Elise's mother. "Please make sure everyone stays here until I come back."

"Of course, Officer," she replied.

I let Vinnie lead the way back to the first floor and stayed silent as he squared his shoulders and returned to the chapel. I watched him stride up the aisle, drawing the eye of everyone gathered there.

"Ladies and gentlemen, I am sorry to have to inform you, but the groom has been found dead."

"Dead?" "How?" "Where?" A cacophony of voices filled the space, making my ears hurt.

Tania edged toward me from the back of the chapel. I was surprised to see Chief Hayes and Maggie still remained absent from the gathered masses. "Please tell me you don't know anything about this," my landlady hissed in my ear.

"I'm afraid I do. Maggie found the body," I answered. "Vinnie just notified the bride. Chief Hayes is taking Maggie's statement now."

"I know this is going to seem inconvenient, but we will need to take statements from everyone," Vinnie's voice cut across the chatter around us.

"*Por favor* do not get involved," Tania said.

Before I could promise her that I'd stay out of this one, someone cleared their throat behind us. I turned to find Chief Hayes standing there. "We need to have a chat, Miss Ingram."

A lump formed in my throat as I cast Tania a panicked look. Only there was nothing she could do for me. I followed the police chief out into the entryway and did my best not to appear nervous.

"Show me your arm."

Oh, how I wanted to tell him I had no bloody idea what he was on about. But clearly Maggie had admitted her concern for my well-being. I shouldn't have doubted that information would come to light. Maggie wasn't one to lie.

I rolled up my right sleeve to show the bruise that was now an ugly purplish yellow color. "I swear, I had nothing to do with this."

"Tell me what happened."

I wanted to protest that I shouldn't have to give this information in a public place, but I realized that he and Vinnie had the unenviable job of interviewing everyone currently packed into the church. He couldn't leave.

I blew out a breath. "I was helping last night at the rehearsal dinner. Tania and I both were. The catering staff had called out sick. Anyway, I was bringing around some wine and Andrew just grabbed my arm to get my attention. I didn't think anything of it. Didn't even realize it was bruised until this morning."

"So, you don't believe he tried to hurt you?"

"Why would he?" I countered. "Honestly, he was

a bit drunk, so he likely didn't know his own strength."

"I see."

"Tell me what happened when you found Maggie," he continued, pulling out a notepad and pen.

"She'd told me she was headed to the loo. It seemed like she was gone awhile, so I went to find her. She was down there. She'd found Andrew and froze. Can't blame her."

"And Miss Ingram, you did not touch the body?"

"No. Maggie told me she couldn't feel a pulse and he wasn't moving. We were down there maybe five minutes before we came to get you."

"You didn't notice anything else?" The way his gaze narrowed made my stomach twist in knots.

"We both smelled something floral, but for all I know it's the cleaner they use here. Didn't seem that important."

"And you didn't notice anything about her hands; like how she wound up with those marks on her fingers?"

Oh, bloody hell.

"She told me she'd tried to loosen the cords around his neck...to help him."

"You'll need to come down to the station later to sign your statement, but for now you are free to go."

I needed to find Maggie. I found her sitting on the front steps outside, her wrists bound together in front of her in handcuffs.

"What's this?" I demanded.

Maggie looked up, unshed tears in her eyes. "No one else was there, Darcy. And my head's a bit fuzzy. I must have tried to help him, but I don't remember. I can't explain why else I would have touched him. It looks bad."

"You didn't do anything. I know in my gut you didn't do this. I'm going to prove it."

"For the record, this was not how I expected our first date to go," Maggie blurted.

I smiled in spite of myself. "Me either. I wish I could explain what happened."

"I still can't shake the weird compulsion I had to go down there. It was like the universe needed me to know."

"We can go talk to Beau. Maybe he can clear things up." Or at least the chameleon might shed a little light on whether he could even reach someone from that distance.

"Maybe," Maggie murmured. "That's assuming Rick would let me out of these cuffs anytime soon."

"I still can't believe anyone would want Andrew dead," I sighed. "I mean, sure he was a bit pompous and bragged last night about the fact he won Casey over, but I can't believe someone would begrudge him being proud of his bride-to-be."

Maggie didn't respond. Her silence filled the dead air between us, making it almost claustrophobic. The doors behind us opened and other attendees began trickling out, all whispering to each other about the tragic nature of Andrew's demise. I immediately peeled off my jacket and hung it over Maggie's wrists as best I could without getting any of the blood on the fabric. One woman even bemoaned how she hoped the shock didn't give Gerry a heart attack.

"Where were his groomsmen and Gerry?" I blurted.

"What?" Confusion colored Maggie's tone.

"You said that Gerry and the groomsmen were getting changed in the basement. But none of them came looking for Andrew. Why is that?"

"We have no idea how long he was dead before I found him. They could have thought he'd just gone to the bathroom. Or maybe he was rehearsing his vows?" Maggie offered.

"Something just feels off about this." I was on my feet before I finished speaking.

"Darcy, you're getting involved," Maggie reminded me.

I knew I shouldn't, but I couldn't help myself.

Maggie was in Chief Hayes' crosshairs this time and I wasn't going to let her go down for something she didn't do. I just had to clear her name and stay out of the police's way.

I fought the tide of people continuing to pour out of the church. Behind me, I heard the screech of tires and then two jump-suited people with a gurney and crime scene tape slung over one shoulder hurried past me. The crime scene techs had finally arrived.

"Darcy, where are you going?" Tania caught my elbow as I started toward the chapel.

"Do you know if they notified Gerry and the groomsmen?"

"Not unless Rick did it before he came back in. He's been taking statements for the last twenty minutes, same as Vinnie."

"I can't shake this feeling that something's off," I told her. "Is that the only way down to the basement?" I gestured to the stairs now blocked by yellow tape.

Tania took a deep breath to compose herself before she nudged me to the left. "You can get down there this way."

No one paid us any attention as we took the far stairs that led to the basement. Our footsteps echoed on the cement flooring and I fought back a shiver. As

Tania led the way past a storage closet, I got the impression this space wasn't used often. It surprised me that Andrew had agreed to get ready for his wedding down here. Wouldn't it have been more comfortable to do so elsewhere and then just come over? I could ask Gerry or the groomsmen when we found them.

"I believe they were getting ready in here," Tania explained and stopped at a closed door. "They used to host after service luncheons down here."

Knocking on the door didn't draw the attention I hoped. In fact, I couldn't hear any sounds from within. Even if they weren't concerned about Andrew's whereabouts, they'd be chatting amongst themselves.

"Hello? Can we come in?" I called.

"Gerry, it's Tania," Tania added.

Still nothing.

We shared a worried look before I reached for the doorknob and turned it. The door swung inward on aging hinges, but even the loud squeak wasn't enough to elicit a response.

The room was dimly lit as we stepped in. I found the switch beside the door easily enough and flipped it on. The lack of response became horrifyingly evident as the bulbs above us illuminated the space.

Gerry and the two groomsmen lay sprawled on the furniture, passed out.

I didn't bother to consider the consequences of my actions. I raced to Gerry first and pressed my fingers to his throat. His pulse thrummed along at a steady clip. He wasn't dead.

"We need an ambulance," I called to Tania as I moved to check the other men.

First Andrew turned up dead. Now the groomsmen and Gerry were out cold. What was going on?

6

———

Adrenaline kept me from completely falling apart as I watched Tania dig into her purse for her phone. Everything moved in slow motion. I bent over Gerry's prone form. His left hand hung over the edge of the chair. A half-empty cup of coffee lay spilled on the floor. His head was lolled back, mouth agape. I thought I heard rasping breaths from him and I gently propped his head forward.

"Come on, Gerry, wake up," I urged.

Footsteps thundered in the hallway beyond the room and I looked up to find both Chief Hayes and Vinnie come skidding to a halt.

"Damn it." Chief Hayes couldn't keep the curse from slipping out.

"We just found them," I explained. "They seem to still be breathing."

"Yes, we need paramedics at the church. Three men need assistance," Tania said, phone pressed to her ear. "I don't know. We found them unconscious."

Chief Hayes moved past Tania into the room and knelt beside the bearded groomsman. He had a stain on his dark blue tie that trailed onto the matching cummerbund. From this distance it looked like jam. A cursory glance around the room didn't reveal anything obvious. I didn't even see any food or drink aside from the one staining the floor beneath Gerry's chair. That detail felt important, but I couldn't piece together why.

I closed my eyes and tried to recall what the detail might be, when the image of the flower petal pressed into Andrew's jacket filled my mind's eye. I still stood by Gerry's prone form, hand supporting his head. His breathing had turned less raspy at least. That had to be a good sign. I spotted the boutonniere in his jacket lapel, a single violet. The groomsmen all sported matching ones. *Where did the white petal come from*?

"We need to check on the bridal party. Now," Chief Hayes ordered Vinnie.

The deputy took off at a sprint, leaving Tania and I alone with the chief and the three unconscious men. It seemed an interminable length of time before anyone spoke again.

"I would have thought you'd gone home." Chief Hayes directed his words to me.

"I'm glad I didn't," I retorted.

He didn't disagree with my statement. Instead, he took a few steps back to survey the whole scene. He didn't have time to say anything else before more footfalls announced the paramedics' presence. With their arrival, Chief Hayes ushered Tania and I out of the space to supervise their revival efforts.

I did linger long enough to hear Chief Hayes answer his phone. "Give me some good news."

The way the tension fled his shoulders suggested whoever was on the other end—my guess was Vinnie—the bridal party was unharmed. Whatever was going on here, it appeared targeted towards Andrew and his entourage. It still begged the question of who would want to cause the man harm? Had whoever done it gone after Gerry and the others to keep them out of the way?

"We should get back to the B&B. I'm sure guests will want somewhere to gather," Tania said, falling into her hostess persona.

"Not a bad idea. I need to stop by Maggie's," I replied, remembering I wanted to check on Beau and try to understand what had compelled Maggie to find Andrew. Something was going on that had ensnared my date and I intended to figure out what.

"Please promise me you will be careful." Tania clutched my right hand to stop me from heading upstairs.

"I'm probably the safest person here," I reassured her. "Most people still don't' know me and whatever happened to Andrew feels personal. I'm the last person anyone would think might be looking into it."

With that, I retreated upstairs. To my surprise, Maggie had remained outside. She was on her feet now, pacing the length of the stairs, hands still cuffed. Her head whipped around at my approach and I saw her body tense for a moment before she realized my identity.

"Sorry, I didn't mean to run off on you," I said.

"I saw the paramedics arrive. What's going on?"

"They found Gerry and the groomsmen out cold. Not sure what happened." I gestured for her keys, realizing too late she had no way of handing them to me with her hands still covered in Andrew's blood.

"I'm going to stop by your place, see if Beau really was the one giving you signals."

"Right. Keys are in my bag," she said and jutted her right hip toward me so I could snag the keys.

After a moment of awkward silence, Maggie said, "Did I ever tell you he almost hit on me once?"

"Andrew?" I snorted.

"He realized pretty quick he was barking up the wrong tree, but one Christmas a few years ago he asked me out."

"He doesn't seem the type to give up easily when he wants something." His comment about the length of time it took to win Casey over came to mind.

"I can be persuasive when I want to be."

"I believe that."

I wished I could just take her with me. However, we didn't need to feed the gossip mill any more than the wedding already had.

My unease tightened my shoulder muscles as I entered Maggie's second floor apartment. I scanned the open concept kitchen and living room for Beau's presence. Nothing stood out to me before I realized that was the point. Even with magic, I couldn't always detect his presence unless he wanted to reveal himself.

"Beau, I need to talk to you," I called.

I waited for my chameleon friend to make an appearance, but he was either ignoring me or off somewhere else entirely.

"Okay, what do we know," I said, talking through the problem out loud, hoping it would be enough to entice Beau. "There was a flower on Andrew's suit jacket. It didn't match the boutonnieres," I said as I paced the distance between the edge of the couch and the kitchen table.

"They had violets in their lapels and I am certain the petal I saw was paler. Lighter. So maybe whoever attacked Andrew had this other flower on them and it transferred when they attacked him."

I sat down on the couch and jumped only slightly when I felt a reptilian claw on my knee just as Beau appeared.

Well, the flowers on the altar were pretty pale. I think they were a mix of yellows and whites. And hadn't the florist been by last night to see about the bouquets? I should have paid more attention to what Casey's bouquet looked like. But her reaction when Vinnie broke the news was genuine. She'd been devastated by the news. There was no way she'd have killed her husband-to-be.

"There you are." I stroked one finger along Beau's head. "You warned Maggie, didn't you."

'Danger in many places.'

"Yeah, you aren't wrong, mate."

I had to wonder if, given Andrew's trail of former spouses, any of them might be a viable suspect. Even if it looked bad for Maggie having found Andrew and had physical evidence on her, I had to believe

Chief Hayes would realize she wasn't a killer. But I had no information on who to look at in terms of ex-wives.

My phone buzzed with an incoming text from Tania, letting me know the wedding guests had gathered at the B&B and she was providing food.

My stomach gurgled on cue. Food should be the last thing on our minds with a man dead and three others incapacitated. My own phone buzzed with a second incoming message informing me that the bridal party had returned to the B&B and ended with a couple of question marks.

Okay, I get the hint.

I looked down at the reptile in my lap. "Ready to come home and help me snoop?"

Beau blinked once before crawling up my arm and settling in his favorite perch on my shoulder. As I pushed myself to standing position, I realized the detail I'd been missing before.

"Oh, I'm an idiot!" I declared.

The food. I knew something felt off down in the basement.

I stopped, took a breath, and tried to corral my racing thoughts. The wedding party was meant to get ready at the church this morning.

And hadn't Elise said something about them doing a brunch beforehand? I distinctly recalled seeing the spilled coffee near Gerry and some sort of jam stain on one of the groomsmen's ties. But there was no food in the room. No empty plates or discarded trays in the bins. Nothing to suggest there'd been food in there at all.

"Someone must have come in and cleared out the food and drinks."

'Suspect?' Beau prodded.

There was no clear motive for Clara to subdue the groomsmen and Gerry, and yet it felt like the right avenue. Besides, if I was wrong, I was sure she'd clear it up quick enough. It was a place to start. I fired off a text to Tania inquiring about Clara's whereabouts.

Her response came back within seconds. Clara was at the B&B.

If I'm off base, we'll find out soon enough

7

Much like the night before when I'd gotten home from Maggie's, the first floor was cacophonous. This time, though, the chattering didn't extol the excitement of impending nuptials. The conversations popping up all around us were subdued and somber. I spotted Ginny in the living room by the front windows. She was providing Casey a never-ending stream of tissues. The poor thing had changed out of her wedding gown, but her hair remained in an elegant up do. I caught her glance at her engagement ring a few times before bursting into fresh fits of sobbing. Elise and her mother were conspicuously absent from Casey's side.

It wasn't hard to find Clara. She stood in the kitchen beside Tania, manning the stove. I wasn't sure I liked the idea of Tania sharing her kitchen with this woman if, in fact, she'd done something to the wedding party's food. I still didn't get why she would want to harm anyone. But I was about to find out.

"Hope this doesn't happen to many of your clients," I said awkwardly trying to get the woman's attention.

"Sorry?" She looked at me with only mild recognition.

"Members of the wedding party turning up dead."

"Oh, right." She gave a hiccup of nervous laughter. "This is a first."

I hadn't expected this to be a repeat occurrence for her. "I wonder what happened." *Time to play dumb and see what she'll give me.*

"I don't know. I was setting up for the reception when the police notified me that the groom was found dead. They wouldn't give me any details." She stopped what she was doing and turned her full attention to me. "What did *you* hear?'

I opened my mouth to answer her, but stopped short. I didn't know what sort of details Chief Hayes wanted floating around in public. "Just that they found him in the bathroom downstairs."

Clara's jaw worked, as if she were chewing on her

next words. "It really is just horrible, ruining that poor girl's big day."

"Can't think of a worse thing to happen on a girl's wedding day," I agreed. "I do wonder what he was doing in the loo, though. I'd thought I heard him and his mates say they were all getting ready together."

"No idea." Clara rubbed at the nape of her neck. "I should really go check on the guests."

"What's going to happen to all the food?" I blurted before she could walk away.

"The food?" She blinked at me, clear confusion in her gaze.

"You said you were setting up for the reception. It was a luncheon right? Surely you'd made everything already."

She remained mute for a moment before letting another nervous hiccup of laughter out. "That food. You know, it hadn't crossed my mind. I suppose I should have brought it and we could have fed everyone."

What's stopping her from getting it now?

"Where was the reception going to be again? I'd be happy to help bring it over. No sense letting it al spoil," I offered.

"I'll give my staff a call and see what they can

bring over. You were a big help last night. No need to keep throwing yourself into the mix."

She was halfway to the dining room before I had a chance to ask her about whether the wedding party had eaten brunch together. Then again, if Casey was so big on superstition, she wouldn't have wanted Andrew to see her before the ceremony anyway.

"Learn anything useful?" Sam materialized out of thin air to my left.

I gripped the edge of the counter to keep from physically reacting to his presence. The kitchen was mostly empty now, but that didn't mean it would remain so.

"So much for keeping a low profile," I chided.

"Don't get your panties in a twist, Darcy. No mundanes in sight." He made a prodding gesture. "So, spill."

"You've got ears. You have to know what's going on."

He let out an exaggerated sigh, or what passed for one since he didn't actually breathe. "Yes, I know the groom is dead. But who did it? You've got to have some theories."

"Chief Hayes thinks Maggie's involved. Had her in cuffs and everything."

"Your sweet, lovable Maggie? Say it ain't so."

"Don't be cheeky. I'm serious. I'm really worried he is going to blame her for something she didn't do."

"So, you're going to find out what really happened?"

"Bloody right I am. Now, Andrew's half of the wedding party turned up unconscious even his dad. My guess is drugged somehow, in the basement. Someone clearly wanted them out of the way, but I don't know enough about the man to know who'd want to hurt him."

"He left a trail of women in his wake," Sam reminded me.

"I know. But I haven't exactly had the time to dig into his exes." I spun so my back was to the counter. "I need to find anyone who would have been involved in the brunch beforehand. Something feels off with it, but Clara took off before I could find a way to ask without sounding mental."

"Who are you talking to?" Elise's voice cut into the conversation. Sam blipped out of existence, leaving me alone with the maid of honor.

"Me? Oh, no one. Sometimes I just talk to myself when I'm sorting through things." Elise would know what had happened with the brunch. But I couldn't come out and ask her without building up some trust first. "How is Casey holding up?"

"Understandably she's still in shock," Elise noted, her gaze fixed on the spot Sam had inhabited only moments ago.

"I can't imagine being in her position." An awkward silence filled the space between us for a moment. "I mean, the groom dying is bad enough, but the rest of the groomsmen and his dad all taken off to hospital. That's got to be even worse."

"They all seemed fine when we split off to get ready," Elise said, smoothing the fabric of the blouse she now wore in lieu of her bridesmaid's dress.

"Clara mentioned something about a brunch this morning. You didn't see them then?"

"We took our food in the room upstairs and they did the same in the basement. Not wanting to see the bride before the wedding and all that. Casey is big on tradition."

So, someone could have tampered with the food sent down to the groom and his entourage. But who?

"I hope you are all feeling okay."

"You don't have to worry about us. We take care of each other," Elise retorted.

"Right. Well, I'll let you get back to Casey. I'm sure she needs her best mate for support."

As if on cue, a loud sob echoed from the living room and Elise scampered off to tend to the distraught bride. That left me alone in the kitchen again. Time to try and take stock of what I knew so far.

An unknown individual had either lured Andrew to the loo for privacy or had happened upon him by chance and strangled him to death. Subduing the others could have been a countermeasure to make sure they weren't discovered too soon. There were only a few people who could tell me for certain whether they were drugged before Andrew left or after and as far as I knew, none of them were presently awake and seeing visitors.

And it still didn't explain the strange flower petal I'd spotted on Andrew's jacket. No doubt the crime scene technicians had collected it as evidence. I was not an expert, but I had to believe Chief Hayes would have taken note of the men's boutonnieres and realized they didn't match the flower on the dead man's body. If I could get my hands on the petal, I was reasonably confident I could trace it back to its source. I'd been able to do it with the piece of vine used to strangle Vera Chase a few months ago and my abilities had grown since then.

I had about as much chance of getting my hands on that petal as I did of winning the lotto. But I did have a legitimate reason to go down to the police station. Chief Hayes had told me I still needed to submit a formal statement about what I'd witnessed.

No doubt most of the town would be coming through the police station, giving me cover to do some snooping, especially if Beau came with me. And I needed to see if Maggie was okay. I hated the thought of her still handcuffed, sitting alone somewhere in a room.

I wasn't quite ready to take my leave yet. I moved through the dining room, spotting Tania offering tissues to some of the guests. The shock was wearing off and the grief of losing one of their own was beginning to hit them. Sure, there had been recent deaths that rocked Brookhaven, but they hadn't been locals. This was an attack on one of their own. *Our own.*

I slipped through the opening that led to the living room. Elise had wound herself around Casey like a protective barrier. Elise's mother was still absent. Ginny had extricated herself from the bride and now loitered near the path that led back to the front door.

"You sure do have a knack for happening on dead bodies," Ginny said in a matter-of-fact tone.

"Wasn't me this time. Maggie's the one who found him."

"Right. Rick brought her down to the station for questioning. And you know, the whispers have already started."

"Whispers? But she's not done anything."

"Plenty of people wondering what she was doing down there in the first place." The way Ginny said the word people conveyed in no uncertain terms that she counted herself among the curious.

I couldn't be sure whether Ginny's magic was on display right now, but I found myself rolling up my sleeve, displaying the bruise on my arm. "Andrew left this last night. I'm sure he didn't mean to, but she saw it and it upset her."

Ginny poked at the skin around the bruise. "That makes sense. She's loyal to the people she cares about. And for what it's worth, I don't think she's a killer. Not in her nature."

"What do you think happened?" My voice dropped to a conspiratorial whisper.

"I know Rick is going to look at family, but with Gerry in the hospital that's probably not going to pan out. My guess, someone didn't want him marrying the bride."

I considered Ginny's words carefully. I'd been operating on the theory that whoever had killed Andrew was after him, because of some sort of grudge against him. I hadn't stopped to consider someone might have wanted to halt the nuptials because of the bride. The list of people I ought to find a way to speak to was growing.

Sam materialized behind Ginny and mouthed the words 'police' before disappearing again. If Ginny sensed his presence, she didn't react. I rolled my sleeve down.

"I think your brother might be here."

Ginny glanced over her shoulder, her blonde hair bobbing against her cheek as she did so. "Probably come to tell everyone to get down to the station for their statements." Ginny pivoted to face me again. "I can see it in your eyes that you aren't going to let this one go. So, I'm going to give you some unsolicited advice."

I swallowed. "Sure."

"Don't stop looking. I love my brother to death and he is a decent cop. But I don't think him and Vinnie are enough to handle this case."

"Uh, right. Thanks."

Having Ginny's blessing to snoop felt strange. We'd settled into some semblance of acquaintance status in recent weeks, but the fact she was tacitly encouraging me to look into Andrew's death felt strange. Did it mean she truly believed in my ability to unravel the truth? Would she have my back if things got complicated? Or was she setting me up?

Too many questions swirled in my head and I excused myself with an awkward half curtsy before retracing my steps to the kitchen in time to spot

Tania speaking with Vinnie. I caught the tail end of their conversation as I approached.

"Honestly, we've collected the evidence we can and I don't think Rick is going to keep her. She's not a flight risk."

"Please tell me you're talking about Maggie," I interjected.

"Can't make any promises that it won't take a few hours, but I don't see why she can't be released," Vinnie answered.

Thank God.

"You know, I realized I need to sign my formal statement," I said.

"You can go down to the station. I'll be there in a few minutes," Vinnie said, glancing over his shoulder in the direction Chief Hayes had gone.

Heading down alone meant I'd have time to go snooping in the evidence lock-up. But it meant I didn't have a usable distraction when Vinnie arrived.

I wound my way back through the assembled guests to find Ginny still standing in the spot I'd left her. Chief Hayes was nowhere to be seen, but then, Casey had disappeared, too.

"You want me to help your brother, right?" I whispered in Ginny's ear.

"That is what I said," she replied, giving me side eye.

"Then I'm going to need your help with something down at the station." After a beat, I added, "It's probably best you don't' know the details."

"You sure you don't want to fill me on what you're planning?" Ginny asked.

"You're the Police Chief's sister. I definitely shouldn't be telling you anything when I'm about to do something extralegal."

Beau clung unseen to my shoulder as we left the B&B behind. We reached the front doors to the station in record time and I had to take a steadying breath to slow my heart rate. Maggie was nowhere to be seen, but that made sense. If she was in custody, the chief likely had her in the interview room in the back. I couldn't risk being seen heading that way, so I'd just have to hope Beau's magic meant to hide me from view didn't end up landing me behind bars.

8

———

I eyed the short hallway that led to the interview rooms and the evidence room. This wouldn't be my first time 'borrowing' evidence and I hated that I even had to consider it. The last time, I'd slipped in and taken a small piece of vine that Vera's killer had used to strangle her. They had dumped her body in the back of Tania's car, trying to frame me for the murder. But I knew in my gut that the petal was important and could help prove Maggie's innocence. Besides, unless Chief Hayes or Vinnie had miraculously developed plant magic while I wasn't looking, there was little they could do with it.

"You're really going all in for Maggie."

"Yeah, well, she means a lot to me. And I don't want to miss the chance to be happy, if that makes any sense." It almost felt selfish worrying about my own love life when Casey's romantic prospects had just been torpedoed.

"It's honorable." Ginny turned toward the door. "I'll stall as long as I can, but you better be fast."

"We'll just tell him I really need to use the loo."

"I think I can manage that."

"I'm going to find out what happened," I vowed just as the doors to the station slid open and Vinnie trudged in.

"Ready to finalize your statement, Darcy?" he said, throwing himself into the chair behind his desk.

"You don't look so good," I noted, hoping to throw him off.

"I was just getting used to the idea that all of the death was over," he admitted, scrubbing at his face to beat back the fatigue.

"You can only do so much." Ginny reached across the desk and patted his hand.

"I keep telling Rick we need more people if this sort of thing keeps happening."

"If you don't mind, I need to use the ladies' room," I said, giving myself an excuse to pilfer that flower petal.

"Down the hall before the interview rooms," Vinnie said robotically.

I made my way down the hall and into the bath-room. I knew the cameras didn't extend quite this far. It was the only saving grace I could think of to be doing this again in broad daylight with a police officer in the building. I felt Beau's weight shift on my left shoulder as he draped his tail around my neck to give him better purchase.

"Sorry for dragging you into this," I apologized before I felt the sudden flash of heat and cold as Beau's invisibility rippled across my skin.

'Better to protect friends.'

I smiled even though he couldn't see it. It amused me that Beau considered me a friend. I eased the door open just enough to squeeze through before making my way back toward the area where Ginny sat giving Vinnie her statement.

"You know, I'm happy to try and twist Rick's arm about getting you some more bodies around here." Ginny's voice carried down the hallway.

I held my breath and did my best not to make a sound as I reached for the handle on the door marked 'Evidence.' With Beau's magic in play, Ginny couldn't see me, which meant she couldn't cover for any fumbling I did.

Come on, Darcy. You can do this.

I balled my left hand into a fist to steady my nerves as I twisted the knob with my right. It swung inward on quiet hinges and as I glanced over my shoulder before stepping inside, it appeared Vinnie was none the wiser. I let out the breath I'd been holding once we were inside.

I'd been in this room once before, a few months ago when I'd been trying to track down Vera's killer. Like now, I'd been in search of a fragment of plant-based evidence that I doubted the police could use. The evidence box with Andrew's belongings sat on the shelf nearest the door—easier to access, I suppose.

I stopped myself from touching the box before donning a pair of latex evidence gloves from a box that hung on the wall beside the door. Better not to incriminate myself. Properly protected, I slid the lid of the box open and moved his suit jacket and other clothing items aside as gently as possible. I groped through the remainder of the items, my hand brushing against something bulky. I tugged it free only to realize it was the cord, multiple chains wrapped together, the killer had used to strangle him. The flashes of color I'd seen were clearly now small opaque stones. One almost looked like the ruby red gem I'd seen Courtney sporting at the rehearsal dinner. Except hers had been vibrant. These were dull, lackluster.

Setting that aside, I felt around the bottom of the

box one last time, finally coming upon another plastic bag that felt lighter than all the rest. When I lifted it free, I was rewarded with the pale flower petal. It looked nearly identical to when I'd spotted it earlier. Someone had taken a neat clipping from one edge, no doubt to confirm the variety of flower. I still had enough of it to work with and with any luck, it would lead me straight to the killer.

I stowed the petal in the evidence bag down the front of my dress. Why hadn't I bothered to change before leaving the house? Hopefully Beau's magic could deflect from the decidedly deafening crinkle when I bent over. I eased the door open again in time to see Ginny standing up at Vinnie's desk.

"I'll go check on her," she announced.

Slipping out without drawing attention was easy enough as Ginny's footsteps obscured any sounds the door made. I realized too late she couldn't see me with Beau's magic still hiding me from prying eyes. So, I did an awkward scurry down the hall to the bathroom.

"You can drop the camouflage now," I whispered to Beau as I stripped off the latex gloves. They left my hands chafed and sweaty.

"Everything okay in there?" Ginny called through the door.

"You can come in," I replied and took a step back to allow her entry.

She eyed me and gestured to the obvious lump in my dress. "You can't be serious," she hissed.

"What were you expecting me to do?"

"Not steal evidence."

"I need time and space, to let it lead me to whoever left it behind. That's not something I'm going to be able to do from here."

"You need to get out there and give your statement before he gets suspicious."

I tugged the evidence bag free of my dress and held it out to her. She looked stricken by the idea of concealing the evidence. "You really think I can sneak this out?"

"Actually, I was hoping you'd be able to hold onto it just until Maggie gets out, then pass it to her. I heard Vinnie telling Tania they were going to release her. Just tell her that I'll explain when she's out of here."

"You certainly don't make things easy," Ginny sighed, but stuffed it into her pocket.

"I promise, we'll bring it back," I vowed as I left her standing in the bathroom.

THE SUN WAS SETTING BY THE TIME I'D FINISHED verifying my statement. Ginny had disappeared about ten minutes ago, returning to the coffee shop I presumed. Chief Hayes had returned and disappeared down the hall, only to reappear moments later with Maggie in tow. She rubbed her wrists, but I saw they'd at least let her clean her hands.

"I shouldn't have to tell you this, but don't leave town," Chief Hayes told her.

"I don't plan on it," Maggie answered as I stood up.

I caught her pat her pocket before walking out of the station. The air was cool against my face and I let out a long sigh as we made it to the corner opposite Maggie's building. She passed me the evidence bag. Exhaustion pinched the skin around her mouth and her eyes were profound.

"I can handle this on my own," I said, trying to telegraph that she should get some rest.

"You're only in this mess, because of me," Maggie protested. "I'm seeing it through. Besides, Andrew deserves justice and Casey needs closure."

"I wonder if there's been any word on Gerry and the groomsmen," I pondered as I fished the fragile petal from the bag.

"Vinnie checked his phone about a dozen times when taking my statement. I think he's really anxious about this. This feels personal and not just to Andrew and his family. This feels like someone's coming after Brookhaven."

"We won't let them get away with it. This might not have been my home for long, but it's the first place I've ever felt like I fit and I'm going to do everything I can to protect it."

Time for a little magic.

Like I'd done at the church, I let my magic bubble to the surface. I held the flower petal in my palm like a compass, praying it would guide me to Andrew's killer. My power coursed through my veins, supercharging my senses and my connection to the nature around me. The flower this petal belonged to had been cut off from its roots, but not for long. Maybe a day or two and it still held a vestige of life within it. It was enough for me to connect with and nudge in the right direction.

Show me where you came from.

The petal quivered against my skin ever so gently and when I opened my eyes, I could make out a faint pinkish glow leading away from us. When I didn't move, the petal zipped out of my hand and hovered in front of me. It bobbed up and down for a moment before it started following the pinkish glow in the air.

"Never met an insistent flower petal before," I mused as we followed after it.

The more we walked, the more I felt the magic tug behind my ribs, urging me to move faster. By the time we passed High Time, I was in a flat-out sprint. I couldn't focus on whether Maggie kept up, because I didn't want to lose sight of the petal flying through the air.

I skidded to a halt when the petal settled on the front steps of the B&B. My stomach did a flip as I knelt and scooped it up. By the number of cars parked in the driveway and on the street, Tania was still hosting the wedding guests. But that meant whoever had left the petal behind was inside the house.

"It stopped," Maggie said in confusion.

"I told it to take me back to where it came from."

"Then why are we here?"

I shook my head. "I don't know. But my guess would be that whoever left it behind is inside the B&B right now."

"What do we do? Walk up to everyone and see if they're missing a flower petal?" Maggie scoffed, her confusion turning into irritation.

Not everyone. Maybe I could get a good look at the flowers from the bouquets, but there were only a few people who might have access. But why on

Earth would the bridesmaids or the florist want Andrew dead? Or was the petal just a misdirect? There was only one way to find out.

I placed the petal back in the evidence bag and folded it up as small as I could make it just in time to see Chief Hayes emerge onto the front steps with his sister Ginny on his tail. I angled my body to hide my hands behind my back.

"Where've you two been?" the chief asked.

"We just finished giving our formal statements down at the station," I answered. "We saw Vinnie and figured you've got so many to do, it would be easier for us to get it out of the way." If I over explained our whereabouts, maybe he wouldn't be suspicious.

"That is … actually useful. Thank you."

"Is everything okay?" I probed.

His brow knit together for a moment before it relaxed. "Just heading to the hospital. Gerry and the others are awake."

My heart leapt in my chest. That meant they were probably going to be okay. Which also meant they could fill in the gaps about who might have attacked them and Andrew. But if Chief Hayes was currently on his way to the hospital, then it was the last place I ought to be. Besides, I had a flower to investigate.

9

———

*E*vening slipped into night and the out-of-town guests retreated to their rooms. Though, I couldn't catch Casey or her retinue alone to ask about the flowers. By the time I'd gotten inside, they had all retreated upstairs leaving strict instructions not to be disturbed. And I'd seen no hide nor hair of Colleen the florist.

"Did Clara end up bringing the food over from the reception?" I broached to Tania as the clock ticked past ten that night. Despite the frenzy of the day, neither of us were able to sleep.

"She brought in a few sandwiches, but it seemed like she hadn't started on the food before the service," Tania answered.

"That's strange. She told me she was busy getting everything ready when the ceremony was supposed to start. I mean, I know it was a lunch reception, but she wouldn't leave it until the last minute, would she?"

"Now that you mention it, given the level of preparation she put into the rehearsal dinner that does seem unlikely."

"There's something else. There was a flower petal found on Andrew's body," I admitted, moving closer to her, despite the fact we were alone. "It brought me back here."

Tania sat in silence; lips pressed into a firm line as she considered my words. "I know I am not going to stop you from looking into this. But it seems as if everyone appears to be a suspect to you."

She wasn't wrong. I had a laundry list of potential people who could have done *something,* but no clue as to why. "I need to talk to the bridesmaids and see if it came off one of their bouquets. And see Gerry. Maybe he could fill me in on what happened."

I also needed to find a way to dig into Casey's background. If this had something to do with her, then maybe her social media accounts would shed some light.

"You aren't going to figure anything out tonight," Tania noted. "We should both try to get some sleep. Maybe things will be clearer in the morning."

Morning dawned too soon. I sat up in bed, awoken by the still-unfamiliar sounds of other residents in the rooms around me. Before yesterday, I'd assumed we would get the house back to ourselves by today. With Andrew's death, it seemed likely we'd be keeping guests on through the weekend. Or until Chief Hayes cleared people to leave town.

Any digging I did today would need to be done from my phone. Sage had given everyone the day off to attend the wedding yesterday, but High Time was still open for business today. I donned the brightly colored uniform shirt with the signature marijuana leaf logo before heading downstairs. To my surprise, Tania was the only one up and about.

"Could you do me a favor?" I poured myself a mug of coffee and eyed Tania.

"You can ask."

"Would you stop by the hospital today and check up on Gerry? See if he can recall anything?"

Tania arched a dark brow at me. "You want me to go snooping for you?"

"I'm stuck at work all day. And you are friends. I'm sure he'd appreciate seeing a friendly and familiar face in his time of need."

"And if I happen to ask him about what he

recalls, then all the better?”

“Come on, you want to know what happened, too.”

“I do. I will stop by when visiting hours open and see what I can find out. And for what it’s worth, it sounded like Casey was very active on Instagram. You might find what you’re looking for there.”

I flashed her a smile. “Thanks.”

I drank the coffee in a few quick gulps before heading off to work. The caffeine jolt was enough to jumpstart my synapses. I’d packed the petal in my bag just to be safe. And in case it didn’t yield any more answers, I’d be ready to return it to evidence as soon as possible.

The weather was cool, but I needed the fresh air and decided to walk to High Time instead of driving. It gave me time to think.

My list of suspects was long, but there had to be a way to narrow it down.

There was certainly something suspicious about the fact that Clara hadn’t prepped all of the food for the reception before the ceremony. And from my limited experience with her running the kitchen the other night, I doubted she would let anyone else near the brunch menu.

Then there was the flower petal. The fact that I’d been led back to the B&B where Casey and her bridesmaids resided wasn't a coincidence. Yet again, it didn't seem like Casey had any reason to want her husband-to-be dead. And none of them had any clear motive I could determine yet.

Time to do some social media snooping.

Ducking into the employee entrance at High Time, I found my boss, Sage unlocking the door to the growth room. I could see her eyes were red rimmed beneath her glasses.

"How are you holding up?" My mind whirred, eager to get started on my Instagram deep dive, but I knew I needed to be a good friend, too.

"It's just still a shock. I can't believe Andrew's gone."

"Did you know him well?"

"Not really, but I know Gerry's going to be absolutely devastated."

She wasn't the first person to say that either. And she wasn't wrong. "I'm sure the police will figure out what happened." I hadn't noticed where Sage had been seated in the chapel before everything went sideways.

"I know they will."

"Where were you sitting?" I tried not to seem too obvious that I was digging for information.

"Near the middle on the groom's side."

Not an ideal spot to see something suspicious.

But Sage could be perceptive. "I keep trying to go over what I remember, you know? Did I see something and didn't realize it?"

Sage nodded. "I remember seeing the photographer come in and take some pictures and then she left. I assumed to check the lighting. Getting the lights right in there can be tricky. Trust me, I've seen a few Christmas pageants gone awry due to unexpected shadows."

Courtney was also on my list of people I needed to track down. She'd been standing in the back and I'd gone past her in my search for Maggie. She'd been on the phone, but with who? If she was meant to be getting photos of the bridal party as they got ready, why not just go up to them directly?

"I noticed that, too. Come to think of it, I haven't seen her since yesterday."

"I heard she was staying at a hotel just over the town line."

Now that I did a mental inventory, I hadn't seen Courtney after the rehearsal dinner. At the time I hadn't been focused on where she'd gone, but it made sense she wouldn't be staying at the B&B. There weren't many places to stay in Brookhaven outside of Tania's, though. That would make it easy to track her down.

"I know people are saying Maggie was involved,

but I don't believe it for a second," Sage said.

"Glad someone else believes she's innocent."

"I mean, I don't want to speak ill of the dead, but Andrew had kind of a reputation for wooing women and then breaking their hearts."

The ex-wives reared their mysterious heads again.

"I should get to work," I said, gesturing to the door of the growth room.

Sage nodded and stepped aside to allow me entry. The temperature controlled space welcomed me back. My presence perked up the plants that sat beneath the strategically placed grow lights. I made my rounds, checking to make sure the newer seedlings had enough water and nutrients. A few of the more mature plants were almost ready to harvest.

Once I'd done my due diligence, I settled in my chair and retrieved my phone. It wasn't difficult to find Casey's Instagram page. Tania was right. Casey lived for a good selfie. There were dozens of photos from her bachelorette party. I spotted Elise and the other two bridesmaids in the periphery of many shots. As I scrolled back through her posts, I found when she first announced her engagement to Andrew nearly eight months ago. Their relationship went back another year beyond that.

Skipping back to two years before she'd met Andrew, I found some photos of her and Elise. They appeared to have met in college and had done a summer abroad together. There didn't appear to be any jilted exes in her past. I navigated back to the engagement announcement post and clicked over to the comments. There were a plethora of heart and kiss face emojis from her friends and followers. Many proclamations of 'congratulations,' or some variants thereof. Not a negative or angry comment to be found.

Ginny had seemed sure this was a viable avenue for who might want Andrew dead. For someone who could elicit the truth from others, it appeared odd for her to be so off base. Maybe a visit to the coffee shop for a chat was in order. As I watched the time tick away on my phone, Tania's face flashed on my screen with an incoming call.

"Is everything okay?"

Tania didn't answer. Instead, her phone flipped over to a video call. The Wi-Fi in the growth room wasn't spectacular, but it was strong enough to resolve into an image of Tania sitting beside Gerry's hospital bed.

"Can you hear us?" Tania's voice crackled over the connection.

"Yeah. I can."

"When I told Gerry you asked me to pass along your well wishes, he insisted I call so he could thank you," Tania explained and tilted her phone, so Gerry was more in frame.

"You scared us all," I said.

"Tania here mentioned you were the one who found me and the boys."

I nodded wordlessly, unsure what information he had or not. Given that Chief Hayes had been on his way to the hospital last night, I had to presume he knew about his son's death.

"I'm so sorry for everything," I offered.

Gerry's eyes welled with tears and he rubbed at his cheeks with his hands. One of the IVs pulled at the delicate skin on the back of his hand. He tried to straighten up in the bed. "Thank you for your condolences."

"I'm sure everyone is going to be glad to hear you're on the mend," I continued, trying to ease into my questions.

"I've had a few calls and flowers sent to my room."

"I know it was all such a blur yesterday. Do you remember what happened?"

Gerry sniffled on the other end of the call and wiped at his eyes again. His gaze went unfocused for a moment before he said, "We'd gotten to the church a little late. Andrew and his friends had stayed out most of the night, but they sobered up and were getting ready. Everything was going along fine at first. There were trays of food in the room we were getting ready in. I'd already eaten, so I just had a little coffee."

"You didn't see who brought the food in?"

"No. Like I said it was there already. Then things went hazy. I remember feeling like my heart was beating out of my chest, so I sat down. Andrew was concerned. I remember him saying something about water."

"There wasn't water in the room with you?"

Gerry's brow knit together and he shook his head. "No, just the coffee. He went to get me water and then I … I don't know what happened."

His son was murdered trying to help his father.

But that at least clarified the drugging had happened before Andrew's murder. Clara could have arrived early to set up the food and then come in to remove the food once they'd all passed out. But why would she want to hurt them?

The ex-wives.

I still knew nothing about the wives, but Gerry would have the inside scoop. I watched as the pallor in his cheeks drained from the energy it took to focus on the conversation. He wasn't up for a prolonged interrogation.

"Gerry, do you know if any of Andew's ex-wives knew about the wedding yesterday?"

He shrugged. "We put an announcement in the paper and I know Casey posted about it on her social media. So, it's possible they could have, but they were all nice girls. I don't think they'd have anything to do with this."

"You get some rest, Gerry," I said.

He nodded and sunk back into the pillows. Tania's head reappeared in the frame and bobbed along as she left the hospital room behind.

"There was no sign of the food in the room when Maggie and I got there," I shared.

"Well, I hate to say it, but that certainly seems to lend some credence to Clara being involved."

"There are still pieces we're missing. I'm going to pay Ginny's a visit and see if she's heard anything through the grapevine." And figure out why she'd directed me to Casey's past when the information I could glean from it pointed to Andrew being the intended target.

"Be careful," Tania warned before hanging up.

In short order, my phone buzzed at me that it was time for my break. Time for a little interrogation of my own with Ginny.

10

———

Ginny's was the most subdued I'd ever seen it when I walked in five minutes later. Even in the early mornings the place had a certain energy about it. But now there was a pall cast over the inhabitants. I spotted a few regulars in their usual booths and on their stools at the counter. Ginny occupied her signature central perch, her stereotypically oversized mug of coffee sitting in front of her. The bell above the door announced my entrance and Ginny swiveled on her stool, our gazes meeting.

"Eating in or taking out?" She wasn't usually involved in taking orders. She had wait staff for that.

"Eating in," I answered and she patted an empty stool to her right.

My stomach did a flip as I took a seat beside her.

This wasn't the first time I'd shared countertop space with the woman, but it was the first time she'd openly invited me to join her. She was warming up to me, but it still felt strange.

"I looked into Casey's background and her social media. She doesn't look like she has any people in her past that would want to derail her marriage to Andrew," I said as one of the wait staff stepped up behind the counter to take my order.

Ginny let out a sigh. "You act like what I said was gospel. I'm not the crime solver in the family. But I figured it was worth a shot."

"Which brings us back to the potential for Andrew's exes to somehow be involved," I mused. "Do you know anything about them?"

"Like I said before, as far as I know they're all still alive. But I haven't a clue as to what they do now or where they might be."

"I'm pretty sure the caterer drugged the food for the groom's contingent," I said.

She arched a honey-colored brow and lifted her mug to her lips. "Do tell."

"Well, I talked to Gerry earlier and he said they had food already in the room for brunch when they got there. And he started not feeling well. That's when Andrew went to get some water for him and I guess the killer struck. But when Maggie and I found them, there was no food or food trays in the room."

"Well, you didn't hear it from me, but I heard that the caterer skipped town."

My gut told me Chief Hayes hadn't cleared everyone yet, so leaving town was certainly suspicious. I waited for Ginny to expound on her source, but she said nothing more.

"I need to look into his exes. That has to be the right avenue," I said mostly to myself as my food arrived.

The bell above the front door jangled as it announced another entry into the shop. I spun a quarter turn, just enough to see Courtney standing there. She looked wide-eyed and when she caught me staring, she turned on her heel and left.

I wasn't about to miss this opportunity. I gestured to the plate of barely touched food and called to the server, "Mind packing this up for me? I'll be taking it to go."

I tossed a couple of bills on the counter before dashing out the front door. I stumbled as the door closed behind me and I spotted Courtney hurrying down the street.

"Courtney, wait!" I called, taking off after her.

Without meaning to, my magic rippled out from my outstretched fingertips. The distance between us shortened in an instant as tiny shoots of grass and other weeds wriggled through the gaps in the sidewalk, snagging her feet enough to slow her down. She tripped, landing hard on her hands and knees on the rough pavement. I skidded to a halt beside her and offered a hand. She took it before realizing I was her pursuer and she shrugged out of my grip.

"I just wanted to talk to you," I explained, the burst of magic ebbing as quickly as it had come and bringing with it a wave of exertion and shortness of breath.

"Why?" As she straightened her shirt shifted and I noticed a lack of jewelry.

"Andrew's death is the talk of the town, for obvious reasons, and I realized that I saw you right before he was found."

"So what?"

"I remember you were at the back of the chapel and I had to pass you to go down to bathroom. Did you see anyone else go by?"

"I barely remember you going by me," she said, shouldering her camera bag.

"You don't remember seeing or hearing anything strange? How long were you out there?"

"I don't know, I wasn't paying attention."

"You weren't concerned the wedding hadn't

started yet? I mean, people were starting to get antsy in there."

"Why do you even care? You didn't know him." Her tone turned edgier, more aggressive. She opened her mouth to say more, but caught herself. "I didn't see anything unusual, okay? Can you please just drop it?"

"Maybe you caught something on film? You were taking loads of photos before everything kicked off." Maybe focusing on her craft would get her to loosen up.

"It was just candid shots. Some stills of the floral arrangements. Nothing relevant."

Or so you think.

"Floral arrangements? Do you know if the bouquets matched what was at the altar?"

"I assume so. I hadn't made it upstairs to photo-graph the girls when everything happened."

"Could I see your pictures? Just to sate my curiosity." After a beat I added, "I promise, I'll leave you alone."

Courtney considered my request for a moment before relenting and opening up her bag. She flipped the camera on and brought up the display of stored images. She flipped to the ones she'd taken at the front of the chapel and handed it over.

"I don't know what you think you're going to find," she commented.

I tried to fiddle with the settings, but the zoom feature eluded me. "Would you mind, I was hoping to get a better look at the flowers?"

Courtney took the camera back, tapped a few buttons and the image enlarged. Her grip tightened ever so slightly when I tried to take it back. My heart hammered against my rib cage as I studied each bloom in turn. They were all pale purples and pinks, but the shape of the petals was wrong. On a whim, I hit the forward button to see what she'd captured before leaving the chapel. A few images of guests and the altar itself. I went back the other direction and found a shot of Colleen, the florist in one of the shots bent over the arrangement. A necklace caught the sunlight from the window behind Courtney's position and it sparkled vibrant green. Scrolling farther back showed a few shots of Casey and the bridesmaids getting their hair done, but no bouquets in sight.

"Thanks," I said, handing the camera back.

Courtney stowed the device in her bag and hurried off in the direction she'd been heading when I caught up to her. I stood there on the sidewalk mentally cataloging what I now knew.

The flower petal found on Andrew had likely

come from one of the bouquets. That didn't rule out the bridesmaids and it still made Colleen a possibility. And I was convinced Clara was involved in drugging Gerry and the groomsmen.

Suddenly, a compulsion came over me and I reached into my bag until I found the clear baggie with the flower petal in it. As I resolved to find its true origin, I recalled the length of cord that had been used to strangle Andrew, with its dull stones mixed amongst the cord. What colors had they been again? Yellow, red, green?

Like Colleen and Courtney's necklaces. And hadn't Clara's been yellowish? Even if I was right and that linked them together, what motive would these three disparate women have to murder a man?

It was time to dig into Andrew's exes.

 agony. I resorted to pacing the length of the growth room until my phone beeped at me, signaling the end of my shift. I raced out the employee entrance and made a beeline for the public library. I figured using public computers to do my snooping was safer than my own computer.

I was one of only a handful of patrons in the

library when I walked through the pneumatic doors. I half-expected to find Gerry occupying one of the chairs in the computer area with a paper in his lap. A pang of sadness gripped my stomach as I realized he wouldn't be taking up residence there for a while yet. I spotted today's paper sitting on the table and snagged a copy. There probably wasn't much in it he'd want to read, but he did have traditions to uphold.

I somehow doubted Andrew was on social media. In fact, he'd only been in a couple of photos with Casey on her Instagram profile. The engagement announcement had been more focused on the ring rather than the man she'd intended to wed. Instead, I logged onto Brookhaven's public records database and typed Andrew's name in the section for marriage licenses.

Five records populated on the screen. I hadn't realized there'd been that many wives. I selected the top result to find it was his pending marriage license with Casey. One that would never be fulfilled. The next result was for his marriage four years ago to a Colleen Forrest. He'd married a Courtney Berringer three years before that and a Clara Ramirez-Holmes four years before that. The last entry was from nearly twenty-five years ago to a Catrina Guthrie.

My mind was beginning to slot things into place.

It couldn't be a coincidence that the caterer, the florist, and the photographer all shared first names with Andrew's ex-wives. Could it? I opened a new browser tab, then typed in Clara Ramirez-Holmes and caterer into the search bar.

A website came up for Catering by Clara with photos of elegant food and a list of proposed menu offerings for weddings, birthdays, and other events. I navigated to the About page and found a photo of the woman I'd shared a kitchen with two nights ago. My stomach dropped.

"Maybe it's a coincidence."

Please let it be a coincidence.

Searches for Colleen and Courtney turned up websites of their own with professional headshots of the women I'd encountered. For a brief moment, all of the air went out of my lungs and my vision greyed out.

"Definitely not a coincidence," I muttered under my breath.

A simple search of Catrina Guthrie brought up a host of results, but nothing useful. No images to clue me in to Andrew's first ex-wife's identity. She might not be involved, but it certainly looked like I'd discovered a motive for the other three. Now I just had to prove it.

11

———

My run-in with Courtney proved I couldn't just walk up to Andrew's other exes and start asking questions. They had to know they were suspects. As I walked back to the B&B, I realized now why Courtney hadn't taken many photos with Andrew in them. He would recognize her and that would have thrown everything into chaos. So, she'd stayed on the periphery, camera always at the ready. It was easier to hide in plain sight if you had something to obstruct his vision. I still didn't know how she and the others had found out about the wedding.

I found Sam hovering on the front porch when I arrived. There was a distinct lack of cars in the drive. Chief Hayes must have allowed the guests to leave. I doubted he'd done so with the wedding party.

"You look miserable," I noted, giving a vague gesture to Sam's demeanor. The usual sparkles and over-the-top fashion were as subdued as I'd ever seen on him.

"All they've done today is sit up there and cry," he whined.

"A man's dead," I protested.

"And how exactly does sitting there moaning about how unfair it is, do anything to find out who did it?"

"It's not their job to get the answers," I countered.

Sam's jaw worked as he considered his next words. "All I'm saying is people die every day and they could be doing something useful."

"Well, I'll have you know I've done some digging and found something juicy," I shared. Even though no one else was likely to see Sam, they could still overhear our conversation if I continued at my normal speaking volume. I inched closer to the translucent form and whispered, "I found out who his ex-wives are."

"It wasn't a secret he had them," Sam pointed out.

"No. But I do wonder if he even realized they were the florist, caterer, and photographer for his current nuptials."

Sam's translucent appearance visibly bright-ened. "Oh, that is juicy. So, which one of them did it?"

"I'm not sure yet." I jutted my chin toward the front door. "I'm assuming Casey and her entourage are still inside?"

"I think they were migrating to the dining room for dinner."

Good. If I was quick, I might be able to snag a seat beside Casey and figure out just how her would-be spouse's exes ended up so intertwined in her affairs. The scent of enchiladas wafted toward me as soon as the front door closed behind me. My stomach rumbled audibly as I approached the dining room.

"This is really good," one of the bridesmaids complimented Tania.

"*Gracias.* Cooking is really my second love, after running this place."

I'd started to wonder if my landlady had some hearth magic along with her empathic abilities. No matter the situation, her food was always like coming home. But I hadn't had a chance to broach the subject with her and the middle of a murder investigation seemed inappropriate.

"Maybe you should have had her cater things," the other bridesmaid told Casey.

"Dina, shut up," Elise snapped, wrapping a protective arm around Casey's shoulders.

"What? All I'm saying is maybe then the guys wouldn't have gotten sick."

"We ate the same food and were fine," Elise quipped.

Well, that was interesting and lent further credence to the theory that the attacker had targeted Andrew. Casey and her friends had been spared. I hastily filled a plate and sat down across the table beside Dina. Three seats down, Elise's mother pushed food toward Casey.

"You need to eat something, honey."

"I can't," Casey sniffled. "I don't think I can do anything ever again." Tears streamed down her face by the end of the sentence and she buried her face in her hands.

"How about a nice cup of tea at least? To help calm your nerves." Tania offered.

Without looking up, Casey nodded amid the fresh onslaught of sobs. Tania disappeared into the kitchen and I busied myself with actually eating dinner. I needed the fortification before pressing on sensitive nerves.

"How long did the police say you all had to stay?" I finally broached, addressing Dina.

"He just said until everything gets sorted out,"

she answered, twisting the napkin in her lap. "It still doesn't feel real, you know?"

I nodded in understanding. "I don't mean to pry, but given the comments about the caterer, how involved with everything had Andrew been? I mean, picking the flowers, the food, everything?"

Dina let out a little laugh. "He left it all to Casey. I guess after being married like a million times, he wasn't into the details. He told her to do whatever she wanted. Budget was no issue."

"That was generous of him, especially since Andrew's dad had told me he was footing the bill."

"So, how'd Casey end up with the team she did?"

"It was through connections from around the city."

"From her position at the university?" I remembered hearing Andrew boast at the rehearsal dinner that they'd met at some swanky alumni event. "She must know loads of great people."

"Oh, Casey didn't really do most of the planning. I think she loved the idea of getting married and having the fancy wedding, but when it came time to figure out any of the details, she froze up." Dina's voice dipped lower as she spoke.

I glanced across the table as Tania returned with the cup of tea and Elise's mother forced it into Casey's hands.

"So, she had help figuring it out?"

"Yeah. Elise and her mom were amazing. They made a big list and just worked their way through it. Honestly, I think Elise's mom missed her calling as a wedding planner."

Interesting.

"Anyway, they handled it all. And now that I think about it, we saw a few other caterers and at least one photographer who were way more expensive and I thought they were better. But Casey had the final say and she wanted these people."

So, despite money being no factor, Casey had still insisted on going with the cheaper options. The ones who just so happened to be her groom-to-be's past lovers. Did she know that? Did Elise?

"What do you think happened with the groom's group? Food poisoning?" I probed.

"No idea. We were focused on getting ready. Casey had insisted we not see the guys before the ceremony, even the groomsmen."

"Why not them?"

"She'd read online somewhere it was bad luck."

"Did she have reason to worry things might not go well? I mean, I'm sure plenty of brides get nervous on the big day, but that's just superstition, isn't it?"

"That's what I told her, but then I'm not the one

who has Casey's ear. We were friends in college, but we weren't that close after graduation." She made a gesture from herself and then toward Elise. "Which is why I'm not her maid of honor."

"Elise and Casey do seem close," I noted.

"It's always been that way. They were roommates freshman year and they've been inseparable ever since."

I made a mental note to move talking to Elise to the top of my to do list. There still was the matter of the flower petal.

"Are you sure no one saw the guys beforehand?"

Dina nodded. "Positive. Once we were in the room, none of us left."

"Do you know if the florist would have a reason to chat with them? Check their boutonnieres?"

"I don't think so. Why?"

"No reason," I mumbled, realizing I'd strayed too close to admitting I was searching for the culprit.

"I think we ought to go see Gerry in the hospital tomorrow," Elise declared to the table abruptly.

"He's going to hate me," Casey wailed.

"You didn't do anything, Case. He loves you like a daughter. Seeing you would cheer him up," Dina replied.

"But what if he blames me for what happened?"

"I know for a fact he won't blame you. He was

looking forward to you two starting your lives together," I interjected.

"He was?"

"Told me so sitting right here yesterday morning. So, I think your friend is right. Seeing you would probably cheer him up."

Casey stopped crying at that and wiped at her eyes with the back of her hand. She offered up a feeble smile as she took another few sips of tea. "Then let's do that first thing in the morning."

"We could all go," Dina offered.

"I don't think we want to overwhelm him," Elise's mom said.

Casey turned to Elise who still sat within arm's reach. "But you'll come with me, won't you?"

"Where you go, I go," Elise answered.

In short order, the women finished their food and retreated back upstairs, leaving Tania and I sitting alone in the dining room. I fiddled with the remains of my enchilada as she eyed me.

"What's running through that mind of yours, Darcy?"

"I ran into Courtney at Ginny's today. Well, she saw me, then turned and ran out of the shop. But the point is, I talked to her."

"Do you think she had some insight?"

"She was standing in the back of the chapel

when I went looking for Maggie. She even pointed me to the loo downstairs. But she didn't remember seeing anything unusual or anyone pass by her."

"So maybe she just didn't see anyone. There are other ways to get to the basement."

"There's more. I did some digging on the town registry for marriage licenses. I found Andrew's other marriage records. And Courtney, Clara, and Colleen are all his exes."

"I don't understand."

"The photographer, the caterer, and the florist that Casey hired for her wedding are Andrew's ex-wives. Well, three of them anyway."

"Something tells me that isn't a coincidence."

"That's what I thought. I'm convinced that Clara wasn't getting ready for the reception. I lost track of Colleen the florist, too. The only one I know I saw consistently was Courtney."

"So, you think they were working together?"

"I don't know. Maybe. I think Chief Hayes ought to take another look at the three of them. I mean, maybe they got jealous he was marrying someone half his age?"

"I've heard of weaker motives," Tania agreed.

"And there's still the matter of the flower petal. It didn't appear to match the arrangements in the chapel. And it wasn't the same as what the men were wearing, which only leaves the bouquets."

That piece still eluded me. Tania and I returned to the kitchen, standing side by side as we often did washing the dinner dishes. I turned to set one of the serving plates on the drying rack when a memory struck me. Colleen had come to the house to double check with Elise about the flowers. Had she gone to the bridal suite before everyone else had arrived? Had Colleen picked up an errant flower petal there?

I needed to get my hands on those bouquets. With Elise and Casey heading to the hospital in the morning, it would be the perfect time to compare flowers. I could try to identify which bouquet belonged to which woman. And I still needed to have that conversation with Elise about how she found Andrew's exes and whether there was more to her selection than met the eye.

12

———

I barely slept Saturday night. Every time I closed my eyes, all I saw were the swirling faces of Andrew's exes, combining into a tangled mess of motives and questions. By six o'clock, I was out of bed and padding down the stairs to the kitchen. To my surprise, Casey stood there staring blearily at the coffee pot.

"Morning," I greeted.

My words made her jump as she pivoted to look at me. Recognition slowly dawned on her as she wrapped her arms tight about her torso. "Sorry, I'm just jumpy."

"You've no reason to apologize. You're the one going through hell right now," I countered.

"It all just feels so surreal. Like, one minute I know he's gone and the next I've got this stupid hope that it's all a bad dream and I'll wake up … and we'll still be getting married."

I glanced to the coffee pot on the counter. Tania might be magical with food, but Ginny was amazing with coffee. "I know we don't know each other, but how about I buy you a cup of coffee. I'm a good listener."

Casey offered up a genuine smile. "Thank you. I think I'd like that."

Donning coats, I led the way down the front steps and toward Main Street. As we walked, I caught Casey looking around at the shops still shuttered on a Sunday morning.

"You know, seeing the church was the first time Andrew ever brought me to Brookhaven."

"You never came to visit when you first started seeing each other?'

"No. I mean, I know he doesn't live here anymore, but I wanted to see where he grew up. I begged him a few times to take me for a weekend away. His dad would have let us stay at his house. But he didn't want to.'

"Why not?"

She shrugged. "I don't know. He wouldn't talk about it. He just kept saying that he'd come back here to get married, but that was it. This was his past."

"I don't want to be insensitive, but you knew he'd been married before right?"

"I knew there'd been other women. He was open about that. He'd married really young and wasn't ready."

"It didn't bother you?"

Casey brushed a few strands of hair from her face. "It probably sounds horrible to say, but I was kind of relieved, like he'd gotten his mid-life crisis out of way before we even met."

"The age difference didn't worry you?"

"People thought I was going to be some trophy wife, but that's not at all what we had. He loved me. He supported my ambitions and interests. Andrew wanted to see me succeed, and have a career and life of my own."

"I mean, the fact he was rich didn't hurt either," I noted.

"He could have been dirt poor and I still would have loved him. I'm not stupid. I know a lot of people saw him as some rich guy who just moved from one woman to the next, but it wasn't like that with us."

By the time we reached Ginny's, the lights were on inside and someone had flipped the sign to 'Open.' I led her to one of the booths, so as to be more secluded. Not that there were many prying eyes in the place this early. But it was better to be safe than sorry.

"I was helping the caterer out on the night of the rehearsal dinner and I heard Andrew say he had to work to win you over before you agreed to go out with him. Is that true?"

A bleary-eyed server appeared toting a carafe of coffee and two cups. She poured them to the brim without speaking. Apparently we looked like the sort of patrons who weren't ready to tuck in for breakfast.

"I mean, I don't really remember being that hard to win over," Casey replied and sipped her coffee. "But I guess it was a few months from when we met to when we went on our first date."

"You don't remember what led to the gap?"

Her brow furrowed, wrinkling the skin around her nose as her lips turned down into a frown. She drummed her fingers against the coffee mug as she contemplated her response. "I think it was Elise."

"Sorry? Your maid of honor? She didn't fancy him did she?" I joked.

"No. She was worried he was too old for me. But we've been friends since freshman year. We've always had each other's backs and I knew she was just trying to protect me. But it took me a while to convince her that he was worth at least going out with one time."

"No offense, but that doesn't seem like the woman I met this weekend. From what your mate Dina said, Elise was the one who organized the whole wedding for you."

"Well, not the whole wedding. But I did kind of get a little freaked out with all the things that had to be done. The flowers, the cake, the food, the dress ... Oh my God, finding the dress was a nightmare. I was convinced we were never going to find the perfect one." She stopped, suddenly overcome with emotion. "I'm never going to get to wear it."

"I'm sure that's not true."

"At this point, I'd be better off burning it. Even if I want to get married again someday, how could I possibly wear the dress Andrew was meant to see me in?"

I supposed she was right. What did I know about weddings? "Right, of course. I wasn't thinking."

She sniffled. "It's not your fault."

"But that all does sound like Elise made quite the turnaround from warning you off Andrew to helping you plan everything."

"Like I said, she's like my sister and she's always had my back. She knew it would make me happy and she jumped in with both feet."

"Not to be nosy, but did she run her choices for the event staff by you?"

"Oh, of course. We went to tastings together, visited florists. I was involved in everything. Why do you ask?"

This was my opening to drop the news on her about Andrew's ex-wives. But there was still more information I could get out of her that might give me a more direct line to the potential killer. I doubted she'd be willing to open up if I absolutely wrecked her.

"Just wondering," I mumbled into my own coffee. I took a few sips to let the awkwardness die down before speaking again. "Things got pretty hectic the morning of the wedding. What was it like for you?"

"Well, you saw me beforehand. I was kind of a mess that he hadn't come back to the B&B. But I rallied and we headed to the church after we did our hair. We went upstairs to start getting dressed. I remember it felt like forever until you showed up with the police."

"No one else came up to the dressing room? Courtney didn't stop in to take photos while you were getting ready?"

Casey tilted her head to the side. "No. She was supposed to, but she didn't. I asked Elise to check in, because it seemed weird. She didn't get an answer before the police came."

There was still something missing here. The flower petal on Andrew's jacket had to come from the bouquets. But how, if none of the women had left the room. That was a question for another time. There might be a way I could uncover the petal's origins anyway.

"Did you happen to take any candid photos while you were getting ready?" I took another sip of coffee. "I know you won't get to wear that dress again, but I'll be honest, I didn't get a good look at it earlier. I'd love to see it."

Casey tugged her phone loose from her pocket and opened up her camera app. She pursed her lips as she scrolled through, flicking her finger to the right until she found one and handed it over. "Elise's mom got a great shot here."

I studied the image on the screen. Casey was right. It was a great picture and her dress looked gorgeous with a long lace train that pooled around her feet. The dress had sleeves which were decidedly weather appropriate for November. But more importantly, I caught sight of the bouquets sitting on a nearby table. Four of them, one obviously larger than the others.

"The dress is beautiful," I said, trying to surreptitiously skim past other photos, hoping to find one of the flowers up close.

"It was literally the last dress I tried on," Casey replied.

"How'd you settle on the color scheme? I noticed the arrangements in the chapel were all very pastel, but the boutonnieres were a bit darker."

"They were my favorite colors. Colleen did an amazing job with the bouquets."

"Did you take any pictures of those? What she did in the chapel was lovely."

Casey made a grabbing gesture and I handed back the phone. She flicked through images faster this time before handing it back. The photo showed all four bouquets laid out on the table, each with a deep purple ribbon around the stems. I zoomed in to the largest, but it was darker hues than the petal I'd found. The bridesmaids' bouquets, however, were identical and looked like they sported the proper flowers.

Before I could speak, a text came through from Elise and I passed the phone back to Casey. "I think your friend is looking for you."

Casey squinted at the phone and shoved it back in her pocket. "She wants to have breakfast before we go to the hospital."

I slid out of the seat opposite her. "Have her meet you here. They do a decent breakfast."

I set a ten dollar bill on the table for the coffees.

Casey looked at me, a sudden sadness washing over her features. "Thanks for listening."

"Any time."

I headed for the door, but stopped. She'd trusted me enough to open up. I should respect that trust by not ruining her day. Besides, no doubt she'd find out the truth soon enough.

"You know, I'm sure your other friends would love to have breakfast with you as well. I think they'd all like to see you feeling a bit better."

"I'll see if they want to come, too."

I waited another moment or two before leaving her sitting at Ginny's alone. As I made the short trip back to the B&B, I plotted my flower scouring. With all of the bridesmaids out of the house for a little while, it gave me the perfect opportunity to sneak in their room and see if the petal could give me a hint as to which bouquet it had fallen from. Then, at least, I would know if one of the bridesmaids was somewhere she shouldn't have been.

I passed the gaggle of women leaving the B&B just as I returned. They didn't' spare me even a glance as they went by. That was fine, this would work better if they didn't see me. I stayed in the foyer for a moment, listening to the stillness of the house. It was a welcome respite from the frenetic energy that had settled over the place since the rehearsal dinner.

With so few people in the house, I was less worried about being caught communing with the plants. Sure, I could go room by room to see if there was anyone there, but plants were remarkably observant. Besides, I was itching to get some practice in anyway. So, I started with the planters hanging in the front hall.

"Hi there. Sorry I've been quiet," I whispered, dipping a finger into the soil to get as close to both the stem and root of the plant as I could. Its leaves perked up and brightened at my touch.

"Don't suppose you've noticed who else is in the house right now?"

I closed my eyes in preparation for the onslaught of images. I hadn't communed with nature like this since I'd gone in search of McKenzie Lawson on Haven Island a few months ago. Then, I'd been able to tap into my connection to the trees and plants on the island, letting me see far distances to find a woman who'd been hiding. This time, I got quick snapshots as the plant hanging beside me reached out to the others spread throughout the house. They might be different genuses, but they were all connected thanks to me.

An image of Tania in the kitchen flashed by,

followed by one of Elise's mom in the bathroom upstairs. Sam floated voyeuristically just beyond the door, but that was it.

"Cheers," I whispered to the plant before withdrawing my finger from the soil.

I crept up the stairs, pausing on the landing as I heard the sound of the shower start. That ought to keep Elise's mother occupied long enough for me to do some digging.

"Keep an eye on her. Just not in a creepy way, yeah?" I hissed at Sam.

He stuck his tongue out at me, but then flashed me a mischievous smirk. I made a quick stop in my room to retrieve the evidence bag from my dresser before heading to the room Tania had made up for the bridesmaids. I did a quick search for Beau, who had disappeared. So much for my hope he'd give me some cover. As I ascended the stairs, the image of Maggie in handcuffs flashed before me, sending shivers down my spine.

Please let this bring answers.

13

Tania would be horrified by the state of the room. Clothes, makeup, and other travel items sat spread out across the room, as if one person's belongings just flowed into the next. That made my job harder. On the bright side, with how mixed up everything appeared, rifling through it would likely hide my intrusion. I stepped around discarded high heels and moved to one of the open suitcases—a bright blue hard cased thing that belonged in a bygone era. I lightly rummaged through the items within in the hope of finding a name to go with it.

"Oh, come on," I groaned as I came up empty.

I teetered over the edge of the case, trying to figure out where to look next as realization dawned on me. I didn't need to go traipsing through everything first. This whole exercise was pointless unless the flower petal actually matched one of the bouquets. I could figure out the identity of the owner afterward. I scanned the room for the bouquets. Casey's arrangement had appeared enormous in the photo she'd shown me, but the ones for the bridesmaids hadn't been that much smaller. They shouldn't be that difficult to find.

Dipping my hand into my pants' pocket, I retrieved the evidence bag with the petal. I vowed to make a trip to the police station and return it as soon as I had something viable to give Chief Hayes. I opened the baggie and let the petal fall back into my palm.

"Let's find where you belong," I whispered and gave my hand a squeeze, as if to reassure the petal I had its best interests at heart.

My magic came easier each time I used it. It practically leapt out of me this time, coiling like a vine around my wrist and twining between my fingers. I'd expected my connection to the petal to have waned given it had been a full day since its separation from the rest of the plant. Yet it thrummed against my palm like it had been hooked up to an electric current.

Using the flower like a compass, I let it point me in the direction it wanted to go. I took one shuffling step forward before stubbing my toe on the edge of a case I'd forgotten lay on the floor.

"Bugger," I grunted and side-stepped the obstacle.

When I turned my attention back to the petal, I felt something else brush against the nape of my neck. It felt like a rush of fresh air, but when I opened my eyes, all of the windows in the room were securely locked. And even if they'd been open, there was no way for any breeze to reach my neck when I was facing the windows head on.

"Focus, Darcy," I chided.

The petal in my hand grew warm as it vibrated in my hand, tugging me toward its origin. That same breath of air hit me again as I found myself standing above a pile of crumpled material. When I lifted it up with my free hand, I discovered it was the brides-maid gowns.

Even if they weren't going to wear them again, wouldn't they treat them better? I'd never been a bridesmaid, but I'd heard from plenty of people at university that they weren't cheap. Moving the dresses aside, I found the bouquets all lumped together on the floor.

A pang of sadness tugged at my heart. Ever since I'd embraced my hedge witch magic, I'd been more in tune with nature and felt more keenly for the flora all around us. These poor flowers had been discarded like they didn't matter. I nudged the still-tied bunches of flowers into a tight row on the floor with my foot. Each had that deep purple ribbon and it was only then that I realized they each bore a tiny silver letter at the end. The farthest to the left bore a scripted D for Dina. The one in the middle had a letter S and the third had a delicate letter E for Elise.

"Time to see where you came from," I told the petal.

I tossed it up in the air and sent out a burst of magic with it, urging the petal to return to the bouquet it had fallen from originally. The petal burned a brilliant shade of gold in the early morning light as it floated down, landing on the farthest bouquet to the left. On Dina's.

Not what I'd expected. Then again, I didn't know the wedding party all that well. She'd seemed a bit resentful of the fact she'd been overlooked for maid of honor status, but that seemed a weak motive for murder. As I picked up the petal, still glowing faintly vibrant against its paler relatives, something sparkly caught my eye.

I couldn't say what it had been. Maybe it was a trick of the light, but I could have sworn something gemlike glinted from beneath the bouquet. I glanced over my shoulder before picking the bouquet up off the floor. The glint disappeared as I rotated the flowers. As gently as I could, I tried to separate the flowers from being bound together, hoping whatever I'd seen had simply gotten tangled in the stems.

Nothing. What was going on?

That same odd breeze tickled my neck for a third time and I felt it sweep across my cheek, lifting the bouquet and smacking me in the nose. On reflex, I inhaled, catching the dulled scent of the flowers. They'd started losing some of their fragrance after being discarded under clothes for several days. I could still pick up the vague hint of lavender and thought I'd caught that same sort of floral scent in the bathroom at the church. My head grew foggy as I tried to recall as much detail as possible about what I'd sensed that day.

An unfamiliar scent hit me, coating my nose and throat as I inhaled a second time. It tasted chemical and I dropped the bouquet on the floor. My vision blurred and began graying out at the edges.

Something's wrong.

I tried to inhale, but wound up in a coughing fit. My fingers ached from where I'd touched the flowers and my head swam. I needed to get out of the room. I staggered for the door, not bothering to cover my tracks as I groped half-blind for the doorknob. I managed to twist the handle and the door swung inward, forcing me back into the room.

"Hel—" I croaked out before stumbling into the hall and my equilibrium deserted me.

A rhythmic beeping roused me. My head throbbed in time to the sound and I raised a hand to my ear in a weak effort to block the noise. Something snagged my arm on its journey to protect my ear and I managed to open one bleary eye to see thin tubes snaking up over my elbow to a tall stand beside me.

"Easy now." Maggie's voice came from my right and I turned to find her sitting beside me.

"What ... happened?" My throat felt raw.

"You scared us half to death, that's what," she answered.

"The aching in my head persisted. I shifted in the bed—which I now realized wasn't mine—and the movement was enough to send additional cascades of pain through my skull.

I settled back against the pillow and waited for the pain to subside. When it receded to a dull thudding, I opened my eyes again to look at Maggie. Slowly, my snooping in the bridesmaids' room came back to me. Before I could mention it, a petite woman in blue scrubs and a lab coat appeared.

"Miss Ingram, good to see you're awake."

"Everything's a bit fuzzy," I said, touching my temple.

"Mind telling me what you do remember?" She pulled a pen light out of the lab coat's pocket and shone it in my eyes.

I winced at the brightness. "Just that I smelled something strange and had trouble breathing. I think I passed out and then I woke up here."

"You were exposed to a toxin. We're still running tests, but the lab should be able to identify it soon. For now, we're going to keep administering IV fluids and monitor you." The doctor glanced toward something in the hallway. "There's someone here to see you, if you're up for another visitor."

I did my best to sit upright in preparation for whoever this visitor might be. My heart sank when Chief Hayes filled the doorway. "I've just got a few questions," he said.

I wanted to refuse his request. I still needed to get my head straight and fill in Maggie, and Tania if she was around. But I also knew telling the Chief of Police no was a surefire way to get on his bad side.

"I'll try," I responded.

"That's all I ask." His tone was far gentler than I'd ever heard before.

Maggie stood, the chair squeaking against the flooring. I reached a hand toward her. "You can stay" I glanced to Chief Hayes. "Right?"

"Sure."

Maggie sat back down and gave my hand a reassuring squeeze. Knowing she was here for me helped to clear the brain fog. Then again, I couldn't be sure it wasn't her magic that was giving me a boost.

"What do you want to know?" I addressed the chief.

"Where were you when this started?"

"At the B&B."

"Where in the house? Tania said she found you upstairs unconscious near the stairs."

"My room is up there."

"So, you were in your room?"

"No." That ache in my temple returned, making it difficult to focus. "I was in the room given to the bridesmaids. I wanted to see if there was anything I could do. Like clean or something."

"And then what happened?"

"I looked around a bit and then I started feeling off."

"Did you touch anything in the room?"

My pulse quickened, thrumming painfully in my neck and my heart beat triple time against my ribs. Had I managed to get the flower petal back into the evidence bag and out of sight before passing out? If he went to check the room, would he find the evidence I'd pilfered?

"I moved some clothes. Honestly the room was a bit of a disaster zone. Shoes, clothes, and cases, all over."

"Something landed you in the hospital, Miss Ingram." I met his gaze and immediately regretted it. Those eerie flecks of amber in his gaze shone beneath the harsh hospital lights, reminding me almost of the glint I thought I'd seen in the bouquet.

"I think I picked up one of the bouquets. That's when I started feeling ill."

"Thank you."

"Has there been any progress on Andrew's case?" The words slipped out.

"Can't discuss an ongoing police investigation with you." He glanced toward Maggie. "But, we have cleared Maggie."

Thank God.

"Have you talked to his ex-wives?"

Chief Hayes looked annoyed at my question. As if my words presumed he was incapable of doing his job. "We are pursuing all leads."

"They're in town. I thought you should know that."

"And how do you know this?"

"We got to talking about Andrew and I couldn't remember his exes by name, so we looked them up," Maggie interjected with a blatant lie.

"And how do you know they are in town?"

Maggie glanced my way, hoping I could fill in that detail. "We found some photos online of Andrew and his wives ... I thought they looked a little familiar. Chief, the caterer, florist, and photographer Casey hired for the wedding were all married to Andrew previously."

A vein in the chief's neck pulsed visibly at the admission. This wasn't where or even how I'd planned to share the information with the chief, but there was no taking it back now. And he needed to know that information. What he did with it was up to him.

"I see. Well, thank you for bringing this to my attention." He took a step toward the door. "Get better, Miss Ingram."

"Would it kill him to call me Darcy?" I muttered once he was gone.

"Tania told me about Andrew's exes. I didn't believe her, but it's true, isn't it?" Maggie's voice came out in a hushed tone.

"You didn't have to lie for me about how I found the information."

"If you'd done something extra illegal I didn't want you to get in trouble."

"Lucky for you, I used the almighty power of the town's own records to my advantage."

"So, what's your theory?"

"Maybe they're all working together? I mean, Gerry said the food was already in the room when they went down. And there wasn't food when we found them, so someone had to remove it. When I talked to Clara, she had a shaky alibi."

"What about the other two?"

"Well, I know I saw Colleen, the florist, in the chapel around the time you were leaving. But she did leave and I've no idea where to. And I know I saw Courtney, the photographer, standing outside the chapel on her phone when I came looking for you."

"I still don't understand how we could have missed seeing someone coming or going. I know I was in shock, but Andrew was still warm when I found him. He hadn't been dead long."

I couldn't even begin to posit a theory on that one. "I was in the bridesmaids' room, because I was convinced that petal came from one of the bouquets. And I was right." A realization hit me. "Oh, the petal.

I'd had it with me and I don't remember if I put it away..."

"Darcy, take a breath," Maggie instructed.

I did so and the panic receded a little. "If we lose that, we're dead."

"Tania found it with you before she called me and the police. It's safe."

My heart stopped hammering in my chest as her words sunk in. "Good. That's good."

"So, you think one of the bridesmaids was in on Andrew's death?" Maggie redirected the conversation.

"I don't know. But it was like I was compelled to smell them and that's when I started feeling off."

I got a chill as the heating system in the room sputtered, shooting out cold air instead of warm. The gust of wind triggered a sense memory of the wind on my neck.

"There was something else strange. While I was in the room, I kept feeling wind on my neck. But it didn't make sense, because the windows were closed and I wasn't ... my back wasn't even facing them."

"Sounds like magic to me."

"How would that even work?"

"Elemental magic can take a lot of forms. And maybe that could explain why neither of us saw anyone."

"What? Could someone turn invisible?"

"Magic is wonderful and there's a lot we don't fully understand about it. But … it's possible."

"That would mean at least one of these women is a witch. But why would they try to poison the bridesmaids after the fact?"

"Unfortunately, I don't think it will be as simple as getting Ginny to ask each of them if they're a witch."

All of this made my head spin. I'd never dealt with a magical killer before. Not that I wanted to say I preferred mundane ones. They could be downright scary, too. But the addition of magic made me nervous. My powers were growing, but there was a strong possibility one or more of these women had grown up knowing about their abilities. They could have honed them for a decade or more. Could I really expect to go up against them slinging spells?

"I don't know if all of the bouquets were contaminated with whatever it was that knocked me out. But assuming they were, why didn't they get sick the day of the wedding? Someone had to bring them back to the B&B," I said.

"We've got time to figure all of that out," Maggie said, her hand squeezing mine again. "You need to rest."

"There is likely a killer staying at the B&B. Tania needs to know."

"I will tell her. I promise. But right now, you need to focus on you. Get some sleep."

I felt a ripple of energy pass from Maggie's hand to my own. It danced up my arm, leaving a soothing sensation in its wake. It reached my head and shoulders before it draped over me like one of those warm towels they give you after a massage at a fancy spa. Maggie hadn't used her healing abilities on me directly since the first time we'd met. Maybe she was right. Unmasking the killer could wait just a little longer.

14

When I came to the second time, the room was quiet. Maggie was gone, but I felt less rundown and foggy. When I sat up, my head didn't ache nearly as much. As I adjusted my position in the bed, a nurse clad in pink appeared

"How are you feeling?" She approached the IV stand and removed the empty bag from its hook.

"Better. Thanks."

"Glad to hear it. The doctor should be by in a bit with some test results. In the meantime, she has given the go ahead for you to eat if you're hungry."

The thought of hospital food didn't thrill me. I could hold out for some of Tania's cooking or even something from Ginny's. "I'm okay. Though could I get some water?"

"Sure thing. Let me just finish up with your vitals and I'll get that for you."

I let her poke and prod me, taking my temperature and blood pressure. She gave me a smile as she left to retrieve the water. I waited for the nurse to come back and straightened when I heard footsteps approaching in the hall. To my surprise, Dina appeared, looking anxious. She kneaded her hands together as she wavered on whether to come in or not.

"You can come in," I called.

My invite didn't ease her anxiety as she stepped into the room. "Are you okay?"

"Feeling a lot better than when I got here. Thanks."

"I'm sorry," Dina blurted.

"For what? It's not like you did anything." Or had she?

"It's starting to feel like this whole wedding was cursed."

An interesting choice of words, considering Maggie's suspicion that magic was involved.

"You don't remember feeling woozy or sick to your stomach the day of the wedding do you?'

"No. Nothing like that."

"Did any of you touch the bouquets that day?"

"No. They were waiting for us when we got there.

I assumed the florist had come up and left them. We never had the chance to do anything with them.”

“What about after everything went off the rails? Do you remember how they got back to the B&B?”

“It was all so chaotic. The police questioning us and trying to keep Casey from totally falling apart. I think maybe Elise’s mom just threw everything in a suitcase and brought it back to the house after.”

“Can you think of a reason anyone would want to hurt any of you?”

“God no.”

“Did Elise ever mention that the staff she’d hired were connected to Andrew?”

“Connected? No. What do you mean?”

“Oh, I’m sorry to interrupt,” said the doctor who’d come to see me earlier, appearing in the doorway.

“I should go,” Dina said. “I hope you feel better.”

I smoothed the blankets covering my torso and legs as I waited for the doctor to speak.

“We got the results back and it appears you were exposed to chloroform.”

“What? Like from the flowers?”

She nodded. “Believe me I’m as confused as you are. Normally, there needs to be more prolonged exposure to have the symptoms you exhibited.”

“When can I go home?”

"Well, you seem to be feeling better. As long as you check in with your primary care physician, I don't see why I can't discharge you this evening."

I hadn't gotten around to getting a doctor since moving here. I'd need to change that. "Thanks, doc."

"And maybe stay away from flowers for a bit?" she said with a smirk before retreating just in time for the nurse to return with my water.

Staying away from flowers wasn't bloody likely. The nurse lingered, checking something on my chart before she donned latex gloves and lifted my left arm. "I think we can at least free you up a bit."

I watched as she unhooked the IV, still leaving the port taped to the back of my hand. I tried to flex my hand and winced at the bit of plastic still wedged beneath my skin.

"You're sure you can't remove this, too?"

"Until we get discharge papers, we've got to leave it in, just in case. But you're free to get up and move around."

"Thanks."

I'd hoped Maggie or Tania would stop by, but Dina proved to be my only afternoon visitor. I rummaged in the small dresser that sat against the wall opposite the foot of the bed and found pants. I tugged them on beneath the hospital gown and stepped into the corridor.

I took in the layout of the floor. Individual rooms branched off on each of the four walls, with the nurses' station situated dead center. They could see everything and had ready access to all of the patients. I doubted they would tell me where I might find Gerry given my own current patient status. Thankfully, I didn't need to ask. I spotted Casey coming out of one of the rooms. Her entourage was nowhere to be seen, but I doubted she'd be visiting anyone else. I didn't get the sense she'd been close with the groomsmen. I walked the perimeter of the floor, stopping at the door to see a little ID tag on the door with Gerry's name on it. I knocked on the doorframe.

"Yes?" Gerry's voice sounded stronger than during our video call.

"Gerry, it's Darcy. Can I come in?"

"Oh, of course."

I walked in, immediately realizing I'd never brought the paper I'd picked up at the library home from High Time. Given the circumstances, I bet Gerry wouldn't mind missing an issue or two. Gerry sat in the chair by the window. He wore a bathrobe over a pair of pants and a white shirt.

"How are you holding up?" I moved to sit on the edge of the bed.

He eyed my attire and raised an eyebrow. "I should ask you the same thing."

"Oh, I'm fine"

"Most people wearing hospital gowns aren't fine," he muttered.

"Well, if I'm honest, I'm a little confused about something. Maybe you can help me figure it out?'

"I can try."

"How well did you know Andrew's previous wives?"

"Honestly, after Catrina, I think I met the others once, maybe twice. And that was after they'd gotten married. None of them lasted very long."

"Would you recognize them now if you saw a photo?'

"What's this about?"

"Whether she knew it or not, Casey hired three of Andrew's exes to staff their wedding."

"That's ridiculous."

"Believe me, I thought so, too. But I confirmed it. Assuming they all still go by their maiden name. Colleen is a florist, Clara is a chef, and Courtney is a photographer."

Gerry shook his head. "No, that can't be right."

"Have you got your phone? I can prove it."

Gerry gestured to the sliding tray on the other side of the bed. I scooped up the phone and opened a web browser, pulling up Clara's catering business first. I passed over the phone.

"But ... why would she ..." he mumbled to himself.

"Do you know anything about why they split with Andrew? Was it messy?"

"We didn't talk about those sort of things. Truth be told, he confided in his mother more than me about that stuff. At least he did before she passed."

"You don't remember anything about any drama? Nothing that might have made the local paper?"

"No, nothing. God, why would they agree to work his wedding?"

A question I intended to answer just as soon as I could track down any of the women. There was something else I needed to know from Gerry. A topic I'd never openly discussed in front of the man, because while Brookhaven was something of a sanctuary for magical folk, not everyone believed it was true.

"I know this has been unimaginably hard, but Gerry can I ask you something else?"

He set the phone in his lap. "What?"

"Did Andrew know about magic?"

That question broke him. He burst out in tears and buried his head in his hands. I hadn't expected to upset him with my question. And I certainly hadn't anticipated such a strong reaction to just mentioning magic.

"Gerry, what's happening right now?"

Gerry gasped for breath as he tried to compose himself. "I should have realized it was something like this."

"Sorry, I'm lost. Maybe you better start from the beginning?"

It took Gerry another few minutes to get himself to a point where he wasn't hyperventilating. I waited on the edge of the bed in silence until he started speaking.

"I think we both know magic is this town's worst-kept secret," he began. "I knew it when I moved here. I didn't fully believe in it, not until I met my wife, Bitsy."

"She was a witch?"

"Yes. The way she explained it, she could influence people. Sort of put them under a glamour."

"Sounds useful." And something one might easily misuse.

"She didn't use it much after we got married. Well, at least not until Andrew came along. It was a thing to behold the way she could get him to stop tantrums as a little boy."

Magic was hereditary from what I'd learned. "Did Andrew inherit your wife's abilities?"

"In a manner of speaking, yes. It was more like he could sway people to him, draw their attention."

"So, he could what, make them fall in love with him?"

"In a way, I suppose so."

His comment about winning over Casey took on new meaning. Somehow she'd been immune to his powers for a period of time. I wondered what had changed.

"So, you think that's why he married multiple times? These women just fell for him, because of his magic?"

"It's possible. But, like I said, he confided in Bitsy about all of this. She was the one who found him a boarding school that was supposed to help teach him to use his abilities."

"Wait, they've actually got magical schools here?"

"So, my late wife seemed to think anyway."

"Did he ever use his powers on you or Bitsy?"

"Not that I remember, but I was away a lot when he was younger. And once he went off to school, we didn't talk about magic openly. Sometimes I think he thought I was jealous of it."

"Were you?"

"No. I wouldn't want all of that responsibility, the constant worry that people might be doing or saying things all because I'd somehow influenced them without realizing it."

I understood that fear all too well. It wasn't long ago I was fearful my magic would somehow betray me without my meaning to do it. "Do you think his wives knew about his magic? If someone admitted to me they could control emotions, well I'd be pretty pissed about it."

"I didn't ask. I didn't want to know."

"The day of the wedding, you said you just wanted them to get to their honeymoon. Why?"

"Because I hoped that maybe Casey would be different. That he'd actually settle down and be happy. She is a sweet girl, really. And she's smart, smarter than she gives herself credit for."

"You seem to have known his first wife, Catrina, pretty well."

"They met in college and got married before they'd graduated. But it didn't last long after that. I think they both realized they weren't ready for all of the commitments required in being married."

She was the only one unaccounted for amongst his exes. "Did you actually not see any of his other exes in the last few days? I mean they were all around."

Gerry rubbed at the bridge of his nose. "No. You know, I didn't really think much of it. I knew they'd hired staff, but it was almost like it wasn't important who they were."

"Do you think any of them could be witches?"

"Maybe. Why are you asking me about this?"

"Because I think whoever killed Andrew is a witch and used magic to do it."

Gerry stared at me in stunned silence, mouth agape like a fish caught on a line. "Maybe this is the world's way of punishing me for not being there enough for him when he needed me most."

'This isn't your fault, Gerry. None of it. And I promise I'm going figure out what happened."

Just as soon as I got out of this blasted hospital.

15

The doctor didn't come through with my discharge papers until nearly eight o'clock on Sunday morning. I wasn't happy to have to spend a night in the hospital, especially after the realization that magic was in Andrew's bloodline.

"You need to slow down and take it easy, doctor's orders," Maggie called after me as I left the hospital behind.

"No time for rest. I think we're getting closer to finding out what happened," I replied, scanning the parking lot, expecting Tania's VW Bug. Instead, Maggie led me to her car. Tania sat in the back seat. I climbed into the passenger seat as Maggie went around the front to the driver side.

"What are you going to do?" Maggie asked as she started the engine.

"I'm going to stop by the police station and see if the chief has anything new about how those flowers got dosed with chloroform."

"And while you're there, please tell me you're going to return that evidence." She produced the evidence bag with the petal inside.

"I am. But there's something else I need to see."

"Why don't we go back to the B&B, just to regroup," Tania suggested as the engine rumbled to life.

"See you there in ten," Maggie said and took off at a sprint.

"But aren't Casey and her friends still hunkered down there?"

"Nothing says we have to have our conversation indoors."

We bypassed the front door entirely, heading to the backyard via the side gate and settled into the lawn chairs Tania hadn't yet stored them for winter. Maggie appeared just as we sat down.

"So, explain why you need to go evidence gathering under Rick Hayes' nose," she said. Her posture conveyed her skepticism as much as her tone.

"I don't know if Andrew's exes are witches, but I think you're right that his killer used magic to get by us unnoticed."

"I'm still not following," she replied.

"It took me longer to put the pieces together, but I remembered something. Before the wedding, I saw Courtney and Clara with necklaces on. They each had a really vibrant gemstone in them. I didn't see Colleen up close, but I'm pretty sure she had one, too."

"So what?"

"So, the cords used to strangle Andrew had gems, too. Except they were dull, like all the brilliance had been sucked out of them."

"Magical objects are rare, but not that uncommon. And typically, they are used by elemental witches," Tania noted.

"Well, isn't it possible one of them could have elemental powers?"

"It is."

"What sort of magic could one of these necklaces do?"

"Honestly, I'm not sure," Tania answered, eyeing Maggie. "Have you come across them before?"

"No, but I'm pretty sure I know someone who has."

"And who might that be?" I prompted.

"Tyson. He owns the pawn shop at the edge of town."

"We've met. I went to him hoping he'd be able to

help me identify Vera's killer. I'm not exactly his favorite person."

"I'm sure he's cooled off since then."

"It's worth a shot, but do you really think he would have sold them these what … amulets?"

"There's only one way to find out. But first, we need to get that flower petal back into evidence," Maggie replied.

"You two go on. I'll stay here and keep an eye on our guests," Tania said.

Maggie and I retraced the path back to the driveway to her car. I climbed into the passenger seat as Maggie slid behind the wheel. I turned to put my seatbelt on and spotted Beau curled up in the back seat.

"He wouldn't let me leave the apartment to come over here without him," Maggie explained.

"He clearly knows something's going on," I replied as she pulled onto the street and headed for the police station.

"Are you sure you don't want me to make the return?" Maggie pressed before we got out of the car.

"I need to see those necklaces," I countered.

"I could do that. You aren't the only one who can sense other magic around. And I'll be in and out with Beau while you've got Rick distracted. I'll take some pictures to bring with us to the pawn shop."

"All right. But you're taking Beau."

"I'm pretty sure that's why he insisted on tagging along."

"You better get camouflaged before we go in, so Rick doesn't get suspicious and go looking for you."

Maggie pulled the car up another spot on the street and extended her right arm into the back seat for Beau to climb up. He settled around her shoulders, tail draped over one side of her chest. He looked rather comfortable. He waited until we'd left the car to turn invisible, taking Maggie with him. I held out the tiny plastic bag with the flower petal out for her to grab, hoping no one was watching.

We walked into the station side by side and I spotted Chief Hayes standing just inside his office with his back to me. Vinnie was nowhere to be seen. Although I spotted a cup of partially consumed coffee on his desk, so he probably wasn't far.

"Chief," I called, hoping to get the man's attention before Maggie passed him down the hall to the evidence lock-up.

I watched Chief Hayes hold up a finger to whoever was in his office before he turned to look at me. "Miss Ingram. What are you doing here?'

"Well, I was hoping you might have figured out how chloroform got on those flowers? The doctor told me at the hospital that's likely what knocked me out."

"We've tested the flowers and it appears all of the bouquets found in their room were contaminated. You're lucky you didn't get more in your system."

"Dina, one of the bridesmaids, stopped by to see me in the hospital. She mentioned she thought the maid of honor's mum might have handled them at some point."

"That would be the maid of honor, Elise Guthrie?"

I blinked, the last name hitting me like a ton of bricks. "Uh, I never got her last name. But yeah, Elise was the maid of honor."

"We're interviewing everyone who had access," he replied.

"Elise's mum was home when I passed out. I think she might have been in the shower."

"As I said, we're interviewing everyone who had access."

He started to turn and head back to his office. I doubted Maggie had enough time to sneak in, deposit the petal, and get pictures yet. "Do you think one of the bridesmaids was the intended target?"

"Miss Ingram, to the extent that it pertains to your assault, I will keep you informed. Beyond that, I can't—"

"Talk about an active investigation. I know," I interrupted. I heard the distinct squeak of shoe soles on the linoleum and I caught the barest flash of green scales as Maggie moved past us. "It just seems like it might be important. I mean if someone was targeting the entire wedding party, they'd have to be pretty angry about the two people getting married."

"I appreciate your insight, but stay out of it."

I was about to tell him that his sister, Ginny, had asked me to help him out on this one when I felt my phone buzz in my pocket. I glanced at the screen to see a text from Maggie urging me to wrap it up. I didn't need to land in the middle of any Hayes family drama, so I kept Ginny's directive to myself.

"You know where to find me if anything else comes up," I told the chief.

Chief Hayes gave a dismissive wave before heading back to his office. I stopped just long enough at the front door to the station to see Courtney duck back into the office. What was she doing here?

I waited for Beau to drop his invisibility before gesturing for Maggie to share what she'd learned. "Please tell me you got some good pictures."

"I did what I could," she answered and flipped to her phone's camera app. She'd taken the tangled mess of necklaces out of the bag, laid them as straight as she could and snapped a few pictures. I realized now that there was a fourth stone in the mix. Something pale pink or perhaps even a diamond.

"Do you think this will be enough to show him and get his help?" I asked as we returned to the car, heading for the edge of town and Brookhaven's only pawn shop.

"We'll find out. Did you get anything useful out of Rick?"

"He said all three bouquets were laced with chloroform. I didn't notice anything on the dresses that had been piled on top of them, but it's possible they could have been dosed already and whoever poisoned them was careful."

"So, you think the bridesmaids might have been targets, too. Just like Gerry and the groomsmen, but we got to them too fast?"

"Maybe. And I just saw Courtney in the chief's office. He knows she's one of Andrew's ex-wives."

"Maybe she did see something. Or maybe her conscience got the better of her and she's cooperating?" Maggie suggested.

"Maybe. But there's something else, when I told Chief Hayes that Elise's mum had brought the flowers back from the church, he double checked her name. Her last name is Guthrie."

"And that's important?"

"Andrew's first wife was named Catrina Guthrie. It can't be a coincidence. And they were married over twenty years ago. Long enough that she could have had a child since then. Someone who could have gone to college with Casey." It could explain Elise's insistence on keeping Casey away from Andrew. Her mother knew firsthand what Andrew could be like. "It's suspicious is all I'm saying."

"I agree it's weird, but do we even know for sure Elise's mother's name is Catrina?"

"No."

"Right. Well, one mystery at a time. Let's see what we can find out about these necklaces, then we can go chasing down people's genealogy."

16

———

The shop was just as I remembered it from my visit a few months ago. The interior was cramped with a large counter dividing the space. The area beyond the counter looked like it shouldn't be able to house as many odds and ends as it did. And there certainly didn't appear to be enough space for the proprietor to simply materialize like he did either. Magic was funny that way, I suppose.

"What can I do for you, Maggie," he greeted, acting as if I wasn't present.

"We need some help," she replied and slid her phone over the counter for him to see. "I'm sure you heard about the murder a few days ago."

"Who hasn't? Rich man bites the dust before he can walk down the aisle. I'm sure there's some poetry in there somewhere."

"We think magic was used, or at least involved. This was used to strangle him."

"I saw three different women with necklaces and very similar stones on them. But they were brighter," I added.

"So, you think I had something to do with it?" Tyson scoffed.

That was a leap. I watched the way Maggie's face remained stony and neutral. "I know you carry magical wares, Tyson. We just want to know if these look familiar."

He let out a sigh and picked up her phone to scrutinize the image closer. "Yeah, they look familiar."

"They do?" I found myself leaning on the edge of the counter, afraid I might miss his explanation.

"About nine months ago, I sold five necklaces imbued with power to a woman."

"Were they these ones? What sort of power?"

"Five gems. Ruby, emerald, yellow topaz, citrine, and diamond. They aren't necessarily magical them-selves, but they can channel power and when used by a witch who knows her stuff, they can be used as a vessel for raw emotion."

"Like anger? Or hate?" I prompted.

"Or grief, or sorrow. You channel those emotions into one of these and it can be a powerful tool to help get over something traumatic. You wouldn't lose the memories of what happened and you'd still have the lingering sense of whatever emotion poured into the gem, but it wouldn't be nearly as intense."

"If they were being used, would that make them more vibrant? Like they almost glowed?"

"Yes. If the witch who enchanted them to hold the emotional baggage released them, it would drain them. They'd look like this."

"You said the person bought five necklaces. There's only four here," I noted.

Tyson shrugged. "What people do with their items after purchase isn't my business. So long as their provenance isn't illegally obtained, I don't much care what they do with them."

"Do you remember what the woman looked like?" Maggie interjected.

"I may run a small operation, but I don't have an eidetic memory."

"Did she pay with cash or a credit card? Anything that might tell us who bought them?" I pressed and bounced on the balls of my feet as my excitement ramped up. This might actually get us closer to finding out who had killed Andrew.

"Let me see what I can find."

He disappeared into the back, leaving Maggie

and I to wait. I spun so my back pressed against the edge of the counter. "So, how do you know so much about his magical object inventory?"

"Brookhaven is a small town, Darcy, and a witch doesn't always have what she needs to do her job. I've come to Tyson for help a few times when I needed something to give me a power boost."

Her admission surprised me, though I couldn't say why. I'd just assumed the healing abilities I'd witnessed and been on the receiving end were her naturally given magic.

Before I could say anything in response to her admission, Tyson reappeared carrying a single slip of paper. I couldn't tell what was on it until he set it down. "They paid in cash and the name given was E. Guthrie."

Elise?

But why would she be buying magical amulets? Was hers the unaccounted for one among the batch used to strangle Andrew? We were getting closer to the truth, but there were still some pieces not quite falling into place. But maybe Courtney's trip to the police station had loosened her lips. If she'd been willing to talk to Chief Hayes, maybe she'd be willing to open up to us, too.

"Thanks for the help," I told Tyson and grabbed

Maggie by the hand, leading her out of the small shop.

"You think Elise actually bought the amulets?" Maggie questioned as we got back into the car.

"But why would she do that? I mean, she was on board with the wedding. She planned the whole thing for Casey. She's been doting on her the entire time they've been in town."

"If she is in fact Catrina's daughter, what if her mother used her daughter's name to make the purchase?" Maggie surmised.

"Wouldn't Tyson have been able to tell she was lying?" I reminded her.

After my first brush with Tyson, I'd learned that Ginny had cast some powerful magic on his shop that compelled people to be truthful in their dealings with him. That meant if the name on the purchase was E. Guthrie, then it was likely Elise who'd made the purchase.

"Maybe she did it for her mum?" I proposed.

"We need to know more about her," Maggie said, a look of determination on her face.

The fact that Elise had made the purchase, coupled with the realization that her mother was Andrew's first ex-wife, suggested there was a larger motive at work here. Maggie was right, we needed to nail down what would have motivated

Elise to procure a bunch of emotion-collecting amulets. But I also still held out hope that Courtney might be willing to fill in some of the gaps.

"I want to see if I can get Courtney to talk to me. If she was opening up to Chief Hayes, maybe her guilt is weighing on her enough to share that burden with a sympathetic ear."

"What about Elise?"

"If I can't get Courtney to talk, we'll go back to the B&B and regroup." Heading back there meant a potential confrontation with Elise. I wasn't ready for that yet.

WE STOPPED BY THE POLICE STATION FIRST. WE caught Vinnie heading inside with an extra-large to-go cup with Ginny's logo on it in hand. Apparently the cup I spotted on his desk earlier hadn't been enough.

"Hey, Vinnie," I called out.

He spun, balancing the cup in one hand. "Oh, hi Darcy. Glad to see you're out of the hospital."

"Yeah, not my favorite place. Can't get any rest in there. I was wondering, have you guys spoke to the staff who was working the wedding?"

"We interviewed everyone. Something you think we missed?"

"Well, I mean, I'm sure Chief Hayes told you that they were all tangled up in Andrew's past."

Vinnie's brow wrinkled in confusion for a brief moment. "Oh, uh, yeah. But how would you know about that?"

"I was the one who mentioned it," I answered.

He gave a small smile. "Of course. Well, like I said, we've talked to everyone already. And the chief's been interviewing folks of interest. I think the photographer's been in there for a while."

That meant Courtney was still there. But we also couldn't be sure how long Chief Hayes would have her detained. I couldn't just walk in and interrupt his interrogation. Confronting Elise was looking more and more likely.

"Any word on how or when those flowers were poisoned? I mean, you'd want to know if there were other targets for an attack out there."

"We've alerted the bridal party and we've got some officers from a nearby jurisdiction coming to watch them."

That meant a visible police presence outside of Tania's. Both a good thing in case we needed help and a bad thing too. Elise might be more cautious knowing she was being watched.

"Well, thanks. We should probably get going."

"Okay then. I'm glad you aren't out and about alone. You might not have been the original target, but I'd hate to see you get hurt again if you got in someone's way," Vinnie called cryptically.

Maggie wrapped a protective arm around my shoulders in response to his words as we got back in her car for what felt like the millionth time in the last hour.

"We should go somewhere they won't overhear us," I said as Maggie pulled to a stop at a red light.

"I thought the whole point was to try and talk to Elise."

"Not without doing some due diligence. We can't just accuse her of something without having any reason or evidence. And we need to understand why she'd do this."

Without a word, Maggie executed an illegal U-turn in the middle of the thankfully empty street and headed back the way we'd come. She pulled up in front of her building.

"This private enough?"

"Perfect."

I felt the pressure of reptilian claws on my shoulder as I unbuckled my seatbelt. Beau shimmered into view and nudged my neck with his head.

'Stay safe.'

"I'm trying, mate, believe me."

I followed Maggie up to her apartment and settled onto the couch while she busied herself in the kitchen. She held up a teapot and I gave a thumb's up as I opened up Instagram on my phone. I searched for Casey's account, hoping that one of the comments or other accounts tagged in her posts would be Elise's handle. It was a place to start.

"You dive into her socials. I'll see what I can find online about her and her mom," Maggie said, setting two mugs of tea down on the table in front of me.

Finding Elise's Instagram account wasn't difficult. She was often tagged in Casey's posts and provided some choice comments—usually filled with excessive emojis. I scrolled through Elise's page, careful not to accidentally like any posts. She appeared to be something of an amateur photographer. Her pictures were nicely composed, but not the same quality I'd seen in Courtney's shots.

I found a post from about nine months ago where she posted an image of her and her mother wearing very familiar necklaces. Elise's was a sparkling diamond, while her mother sported a pale pink stone. The citrine. I double tapped the image to load the actual post.

"Mother-daughter bonding trip. Loved getting to see where she'd grown up. Cute little town. I insisted we do some shopping on our way out. #magicalmom #selfempowerment"

"Look at this." I showed Maggie the post and accompanying image. "That certainly doesn't look like a coincidence."

"Nope. You find anything about her and her mum?"

"Not much. I was able to pull up her birth certificate and it lists Catrina Guthrie as her mother. But there's no name listed for the father."

A sinking feeling overtook me as a thought hit me. "When was she born?"

"Uh, looks like April 12th, 1996." Maggie's eyes widened as realization dawned on her.

Her fingers flew over the keyboard and she pulled up a different records database from the town. I peered over her shoulder as she looked at divorce records from the court. Her mouth pressed into a thin line as she clicked through several screens until she found the one she was after.

"Looks like Catrina and Andrew's divorce was finalized in early September 1995."

"Assuming Elise was born around her due date, it's possible Catrina was pregnant when they finalized things," I said. "But if that's the case, why not list Andrew as the father. It's obvious he had money. He could have supported her."

"Unless she didn't want him to know he had a child," Maggie replied. "If she somehow knew he had magic and that it was passed down from parent to child, she might worry he'd take advantage of that ability."

"So, we're saying the woman who completely organized this wedding was actually Andrew's daughter?"

"It's certainly possible."

"I still wish I could talk to Courtney, at least find out what she knew about Andrew and his magic."

On cue, Maggie's phone rang with an incoming call. She answered it before I could see who was on the other end of the line.

"Hello? ..." a pause and then Maggie said, "I appreciate that. Thanks." She ended the call and slid the laptop off her lap and onto the table.

"What was that about?"

"Apparently Courtney's left the station and is currently occupying a table at Ginny's."

"They let her walk?"

"Maybe they think they can use her to get to the killer."

"You don't think she did it?"

Maggie shook her head. "I'm pretty sure I passed her on my way downstairs at the church and loitering that close to the crime scene seems a little foolish to me. I'm betting she was meant to be the lookout."

That tracked with what I'd observed, too. She was definitely on the phone with someone when I'd gone by. If magic was involved, maybe there really had been enough time for them to slip away before Maggie and I arrived on scene.

I checked my phone. It was somehow already almost noon. Food was probably a good idea, especially after not eating anything at the hospital the evening before as well as skipping breakfast. It was as good an excuse as any to just happen to be at the only diner in town and if I just so happened to sit near Courtney, then all the better.

"Hey, does Ginny's magic work by proximity?"

Maggie stopped halfway to the front door. "How do you mean?"

"If she's just in the room, are people more inclined to tell the truth? Or does she have to be the one getting them to talk? I mean, I'd kind of assume it's the first since she was able to put that spell on Tyson's shop and I'm pretty sure she can't be in two places at once."

"You know, I've never asked her. As much as magic is an open secret in town, we don't really talk that much about it. But today might be a good day to find out. And lucky for us, Ginny's always there for lunch on Sundays. She always likes to get the post-church crowd. They're reliable, tip well, and her poor kitchen staff at least know what to expect."

Somehow I doubted there would be many people in that category this Sunday, given the church was still technically a crime scene. But I'd been in Brookhaven long enough to know that Ginny was almost always there, holding court at the counter. I just had to trust that she'd stick to her pattern and be there today. Because I could really use a human lie detector right about now.

17

It turned out despite the church crowd not having a place to gather to worship, they stuck to their schedule and sat clustered in the booths on the far side of Ginny's when Maggie and I walked in. Maggie gave me a smirk as I approached the counter, sliding onto one of the stools beside Ginny.

"Heard you had a run-in with some bad flowers," Ginny said without taking her gaze off a group of older women in brightly colored hats seated two booths from the front window.

"I'd say I wasn't the intended target, but I'm not so sure. Anyway, I was hoping you might be able to help me with something."

That got her attention and she swiveled on her stool to face me. "What sort of help?"

"How close do you have to be to someone for your magic to affect them and get them to tell the truth? Is it a direct line of sight sort of thing, or more a general area?"

"You're looking to get that shady photographer lady whose been taking up an entire booth by herself for the last half hour to spill."

"Yeah. And you basically told me to help solve this case. Not that I understand why, but that's what I'm trying to do."

"It works better if I'm the one asking the questions or steering the conversation, but I might be able to whip something up in the back to give you a boost. Give me a few minutes."

Before I could ask for clarification on what exactly she would whip up, Ginny was off her stool and through the door to the kitchen. Maggie sidled up to the counter in the space she'd vacated.

"So, did we answer the question of the day?"

"One of them," I noted, turning slowly to see if I could spot Courtney.

As Ginny had noted, she was sequestered inside a booth in the far back all by herself. She sat facing the door. Not a bad position to be in. It would be hard for anyone to sneak up on her, especially since she'd picked the booth at the very back of the shop with no obvious ways in or out.

"This ought to loosen her lips," Ginny pronounced and set a mug of what looked and smelled an awful lot like peppermint tea in front of me. "Just remember, whatever she tells you under the tea's influence will be the truth, but it isn't like it would stand up in court or anything."

Getting it to hold up in a court of law wasn't my concern or my job. That was for Chief Hayes and the prosecutor to figure out. I just needed to know what Courtney had spent all morning telling Chief Hayes. I turned to Maggie. "Wish me luck."

"You don't want me to tag along?"

"Too many people could spook her. Besides, she and I have a bit of a rapport. At least she kind of recognizes me and we've had a few conversations."

Maggie took my seat beside Ginny once I'd vacated it and watched me carry the cup of tea across the shop to where the wedding photographer sat. Courtney's gaze tracked me and I held up the teacup.

"The owner sometimes offers drinks on the house and she thought you could use one. It's just tea."

Courtney stared at me in silence for a long moment before accepting the cup and saucer, and then setting it on the table in front of her.

"Mind if I sit?" I gestured to the empty seat across from her. "Or are you waiting for someone?"

Courtney's body language shifted, her shoulders sagged, and her posture deflated. "Go ahead. It's not like I can hide here forever. I'll have to face reality sooner or later."

Maybe I didn't even need the tea. "What's going on, if you don't mind me asking?"

She let out a sigh. "I know you've been looking into his death. That's why you wanted to see my photos, right?"

"I know you were married to him once," I said with a nod. Better to lead with the information now. There was no reason to keep it close to the vest.

"You know, she never even knew ... Casey, I mean. It was like his past didn't matter to her. All she saw was their future."

"I think she saw it. She told me she was glad he'd been married before. Mentioned something about getting his mid-life crisis over with."

Courtney let out a harsh bark of laughter. "She *was* the mid-life crisis." She took a sip of tea and I could swear when she exhaled there was a fine mist on her breath.

I glanced over my shoulder and met Ginny's gaze. She gave an almost imperceptible nod. That apparently was meant to happen. "If you knew she was marrying your ex, why even bother agreeing to work the event? You could have said no."

"I thought about it, I really did. I hadn't thought about Andrew in years. I was finally in a good place in my life and my career. I was booking steady work. But then I heard through mutual acquaintances that he was engaged again and it turned my stomach. I admit, I went looking into Casey out of morbid curiosity."

"So, I take it your split with him wasn't amicable?"

"Hardly. When we met, I fell and I fell hard. To this day I can't explain it. I mean, sure he was good looking, but there were better looking guys out there. And richer guys, too. Only it was like I couldn't help but be attracted to him. I needed to be with him. And it was great for a while. Fancy parties, lavish dinners. And things in private were pretty amazing, too. But then, after we got married, it started to fall apart. Like little things I did bothered him. And slowly, I started to realize I hated him for it."

"So, you filed for divorce?"

"He beat me to it. I'd been working up the courage to do it and he served me papers. God, I should have been relieved that he wanted out, too, but it just made me angrier."

"So, why bother working the wedding then if it dredged up all those horrible feelings?"

Courtney's jaw worked like she was trying to swallow back her answer to the question. Could she tell the tea was having an effect on how forthcoming she'd been in her answers so far?

"I, uh, needed the money." It came out strained and I watched her hands grip the tabletop.

"You just said you were in a good place with your career, getting lots of jobs. Surely you didn't need to put yourself through the pain of seeing him again."

"Someone made me a promise that we'd get back at him."

"Did you know the others? Clara the caterer and Colleen the florist were both exes of Andrew's too."

"It's not like we have a support group or anything, but when we were all brought on for the wedding, we found out."

"I'm guessing they had similar stories as you? Fell hard for him and then things went bad and he dumped them?"

"Yeah."

"If you knew what Casey was in for, why not try to warn her? Why not tell her who you were and share your experiences … save her the trouble?"

"She's a big girl. She needed to learn her lesson like the rest of us. No one stepped in and told us what was waiting for us on the other side of saying 'I do.'"

"I don't believe you're that cold-hearted," I countered.

"You don't know me."

"I know that you're the only one to come forward and talk to the police. I saw you there earlier this morning."

"Why were you even there?" Courtney took a smaller sip of tea this time and kept her hands wrapped around the body of the mug.

"Someone drugged me and I was following up," I said.

"W-what?"

"Well, I'm not sure I was the target. A case of wrong place, wrong flowers. You wouldn't happen to know anything about that, would you?"

"N-no."

Lying again.

"Come on, Courtney. What's the point in hiding things? I'm assuming you already told the police everything you knew to cover yourself. Maybe get a deal."

"We were just trying to throw things off. We weren't going to tell her she was walking into a horror show. But if she thought things were cursed, then maybe she'd call it off herself."

"So what, you thought drugging the wedding party was the way to go about that?"

"We just wanted them out of the way. And if it didn't go how we planned, then we were hoping he'd call it off."

"I might be wrong, but how exactly would a dead man call off his own wedding?"

"It wasn't supposed to go that way."

"He wasn't supposed to die?"

"No. We just wanted to freak him out a little. Make him understand what he did to us. Maybe he'd finally grow a spine, do the right thing, and not drag another woman down with him."

"So you wouldn't fill Casey in on what awaited her, but you were trying to derail the wedding anyway."

"We were promised we'd get our revenge on him. I swear, I didn't think it would go as far as it did."

"If that's the case, then why not come clean sooner? Why evade questions?"

Courtney let out another harsh laugh. "Oh, come on. You really think I don't know that even with a deal I'm facing serious jail time."

"But you did come forward, right?"

"After the fact. Once it had all gone off the rails and to hell. That won't make much difference. I'm still an accomplice to murder."

"I'm guessing this is what you told Chief Hayes this morning."

"He's verifying my story now, but once he does, he'll be taking me into custody. He told me to come here and wait for him."

"I don't know what magic you worked on him, but I've never gotten him to be that trusting when he thought I was involved in something shady."

Courtney lifted the mug in Ginny's direction. "Something tells me he trusts her to keep an eye on me."

"Now that I believe."

The pieces were coming into place. If Courtney and the others had figured out they were all members of the very exclusive ex-wives club, they had to know about Catrina, too. And Elise.

"Did you know anything about Andrew's first wife, Catrina?"

"You mean, was she involved?" Courtney pulled one hand off the mug to rake her fingers through her hair. "I don't even know why I'm telling you this, but I met her for the first time when they came asking about my services for the wedding. I knew her name sounded familiar, so I looked her up online afterward."

"Did she bring you all together?"

"You could say that."

There was still more I needed to know. Was Courtney magically inclined? What about Clara or Colleen? And what about the necklaces? If they hadn't intended for Andrew to end up dead then why give up the necklaces?

Too bad the conversation ended when the doors to the coffee shop opened and Courtney stood up without a word, leaving the mug behind. I caught the chief's reflection in a picture hanging on the wall as he led Courtney out of the shop. At least she wasn't cuffed in public. Maybe that meant her accomplices didn't know she'd turned on them yet.

Maggie slid into Courtney's empty seat and pushed the mug of tea aside. "Well? What did she have to say?"

"She admitted she knew about Clara and Colleen. She also admitted to meeting Catrina when she and Elise brought Casey by to hire her. Apparently they were just trying to scare Andrew, hoping he'd call off the wedding. Or that Casey would do it if things went awry. My guess is they intended to knock out the bridesmaids, too on the day, but Andrew's murder derailed their plan."

"So, killing him wasn't the goal?'

"Not according to Courtney. But there's still more to the story we're missing. And I think the only way we are going to fill in those gaps is to confront Catrina and Elise."

"Good thing we've got home field advantage," Maggie said with a smirk.

"How's that?"

"You may have only lived here a short time, but the B&B is your home. And you've been cultivating every plant in that house for weeks. You know them, they trust you and they respond to you. Something tells me that if you need them, they'll be on hand for a witch fight."

I wasn't looking forward to slinging magic about. It had nearly worn me out the last time I'd done it on Haven Island and I'd practically destroyed a boat when I'd called on plants to defend me. But maybe, just maybe, I'd get lucky and Tania's B&B would be in tact when this was all over.

18

———

As expected, a police car sat out in front of the B&B. Two uniformed officers occupied the vehicle, although neither looked particularly engaged in the assignment. As I walked up the front steps, I felt Maggie grab my wrist.

"Before you do anything rash, you should probably tell Tania what's going on."

She was right. I owed my friend an explanation before things went badly with our remaining guests. I made my way into the kitchen, but found it empty. A search of the rest of the first floor revealed no sign of Tania either.

"She's out back," Sam said, popping into existence beside me.

"Thanks," I said and made for the back door, leading to the yard.

Maggie trailed me and I could feel her nervous energy as we stepped onto the grass. Tania sat in one of the chairs we'd occupied not long ago.

"We need to talk," I called.

Tania looked up from the book she'd been reading, setting it in her lap. "What's happened?"

"Had a somewhat enlightening chat with Courtney, the photographer. She, Clara, and Colleen were all approached by Catrina, Andrew's first ex-wife. They thought they were just going to scare him into calling off the wedding. Or ruin things enough to make Casey do it."

"Murder was never their intention," Maggie offered.

"Except, I think it might have been someone's intention. In all of this, we haven't actually talked to Catrina," I noted. "In fact, she's been conspicuously absent for a lot of the aftermath."

"Well, she's been inside all morning with Casey and the bridesmaids. Naturally, they are all a little worried about the dosed flowers."

"And there's more. Tyson confirmed he sold five necklaces like the ones used to strangle Andrew to Elise about nine months ago. I even found a photo of her and her mum wearing two of them." One other piece of Elise's post came to mind. "She said her mum was from Brookhaven. When she posted the picture it was about getting to see where Catrina grew up. Is it possible she is a witch, too?"

"The name doesn't ring any bells for me, but we aren't that far apart in age. I wasn't as aware of what was going on around town as I am now," Tania admitted.

"Maybe it was Catrina who pushed Casey to have the wedding here, where she felt most in control of her magic? If she grew up with it, honing it, she'd feel like this would give her an advantage," I explained.

"And you want to confront her," Tania sighed.

"Want is a strong word. I don't have proof that they actually did the deed, because no one saw them. But my gut tells me they're the missing link. And I'm not sure that Chief Hayes would believe me if I told him how I came by the information."

"So you'd rather get them to confess with him present?"

I shrugged. "Well, it worked with Vera's killer."

"It's also incredibly dangerous," Tania reminded me.

"Believe me, I know. I don't know that I'm strong enough to face off against Catrina, but I feel like I don't have a choice. I've come this far."

"Well then you'd better loop in Rick and Vinnie," Tania replied.

I wasn't looking forward to that conversation, but she was right. It wouldn't do any good to get a confession out of Catrina if it wasn't useable. But I also needed to know what I was walking into inside.

"Have you gotten any strong emotions off of them in there?"

Tania gave me a tired smile. "Why do you think I am sitting out here trying to focus on something else? Their emotions are all running high in there."

Why hadn't I thought about that before? Ginny might be a human lie detector, but Tania could sense a person's guilt from across a room. If I hadn't been so focused on Maggie, maybe I'd have remembered that Tania could have been a bigger help.

I've been a terrible friend, letting her suffer in silence.

"Anyone in particular feeling guilty about murdering the groom?"

"I have been trying very hard to block it out. I know I put on a brave face for everyone, but Casey's grief on Friday nearly made me faint. It was so deep, so profound I felt it in my bones. I still feel it now, even as she's starting to transition from the shock and heartbreak to anger. In some ways, it's worse, because she doesn't have someone to direct that anger toward."

Just what I didn't need, an emotionally volatile former bride.

"I'm sorry that's been so overwhelming. I wish you'd said something." I put a hand on Tania's shoulder to show my support.

"You were so focused on what you were doing. I didn't want to be a burden."

"You should have come to me," Maggie interjected. "I could have given you something to block or at least lessen the intensity."

Tania set her book aside and stood up to face Maggie and me. "I know you would have, if I'd asked. But I could feel your own fear that your magic might have failed Andrew and I didn't want to burden you."

Maggie's jaw dropped at Tania's words. If I were in her shoes, I would have denied that hesitation had been there, even if I would have been lying to myself. Which was probably why Maggie didn't argue with Tania's assessment. I appreciated the pair of them admitting their feelings, but it wasn't going to help me prepare to face off against Catrina.

"Is there any chance you'd be able to get a read on how Catrina is feeling right now?"

"I don't want you to risk your safety, so yes. I will see what I can find," Tania agreed and led our trio back into the kitchen.

To Maggie I said, "Do you think you could find a way to get the rest of the bridesmaids and Casey out of the house? They don't need to get caught in the crossfire."

"I can try."

My palms grew slick with sweat as I waited for Tania to get a sense of Catrina's emotional state. I also realized in that moment I had no clear plan of what I'd do once I confronted her. I knew little about how her magic worked and that made it more difficult to mount a counter attack.

"She's in her room, feeling ... calm," Tania whispered.

"She doesn't think we know anything?" I couldn't believe she had no idea what was transpiring around her.

"She is also feeling confident, but about what I can't say."

Normally I loved a confident woman. Right now, I would have taken a timid, unsure girl.

I took a step toward the front of the house and stopped. I pivoted to Maggie and said, "Can I see the photo of the necklaces from evidence again?"

"Sure. But why?"

"Just a hunch," I murmured as she handed over the device.

I zoomed in as much as I could on the cluster of gems at the center. The fourth gem was definitely the paler pink stone I'd seen on Catrina's neck. That still left the diamond one Elise had been wearing in the Instagram photo. I hadn't seen her wearing it the last few days. A tiny voice in the back of my head warned that it wasn't a coincidence.

"I need to check Elise's room first to find that last necklace." I could understand why she bought the necklaces for the other four women, but why would she need one for herself? I hadn't seen Catrina wearing anything either. Then again, I'd crossed paths with her so infrequently and she'd made sure to avoid the people in town who might recognize her, like Ginny and Gerry.

"What about Vinnie and Rick?" Tania called when I handed the phone back to Maggie and made my way out of the kitchen.

"Call them and fill them in," I answered and bounded up the stairs.

Catrina's room was empty when I reached the top floor. I'd heard muffled voices coming from the bridesmaids' room on my way up and I prayed that Maggie would find a way to distract them.

Hadn't Tania said Catrina was up here?

The thought that the woman could turn invisible made my skin crawl and I jumped at the sound of the heat kicking on at the baseboards. I needed to focus and find the necklace. I had to assume that Catrina had orchestrated everything from behind the scenes, using the other women as her cover. Maybe she'd used Elise's necklace for cover, too.

The room was immaculate, so unlike the bridesmaids' disaster zone. The bed was neatly made and the case which I'd offered to take up sat at the foot of the bed, zipped up. There appeared to be no personal items sitting out on the side table or on top of the short chest of drawers against the far wall.

I slid the top drawer open anyway to find it empty, save the tiny bag of potpourri Tania left inside to keep things smelling fresh. The other two drawers revealed barren interiors as well. I moved to the side table and found a mobile phone secreted away in the back of the drawer.

"Please don't be locked," I breathed as I tugged my sleeves down over my hands and hit the Home button. A photo of Catrina and Elise appeared on screen, the same one as Elise's social media post, except it had been zoomed in on their faces. You couldn't make out the gems around their necks. But I could still see the periphery of Tyson's shop in the background.

Thankfully, the phone wasn't locked and I scanned through her contacts and texts. Nothing jumped out at me. Then again, according to her email signature, she was a successful researcher, so she wasn't an idiot. She wouldn't leave evidence lying about for anyone to find. Which begged the question: why leave an unlocked phone in a drawer when she knew there was a murder investigation unfolding around her?

A sense of foreboding crept up my spine and settled just below my hairline on the nape of my neck. It distinctly felt like someone was watching me, but when I did a slow circle, there was no one in the room with me. I set the phone back in the drawer and eased it shut again before taking a deep breath and reaching for my magic. I needed to know if I was alone in the room or not.

There were plants on every floor of this house and I could feel them awaken to my magic. Tending to them and encouraging their growth had bonded us. Perhaps Tania had been expecting something like this—a need to rely on this network hidden in plain sight.

The leaves of a nearby fern bristled and I caught the barest flash of Catrina standing in the room alone. She looked hazy and I realized she must have been using her own powers to keep herself hidden. Then, in this hazy plant memory, I saw Elise walk in and the gem at her throat blinded me.

"They're getting closer," Elise said.

"There were no witnesses. They will soon deem it an unsolved case," Catrina replied.

"That woman is still looking for answers. There's power there I can feel it," Elise continued.

"Let her look. She won't find the answers she's looking for." She gestured to the necklace around Elise's neck. "Especially if you hide that."

The conversation dissipated, but that sense of foreboding remained. How I wished Beau were here. He'd be able to tell me if someone else was in the room with me. Or if I'd have convinced Tania to come along. But I felt guilty enough about neglecting her feelings and the emotional trauma she'd endured. Instead, I'd just barreled off into potential danger alone.

But maybe it didn't matter since there was nothing here to find. If Catrina had told Elise to hide the necklace, she wouldn't have left it here. The safer option would have been amongst the chaos of the bridesmaids' room.

"Please have cleared them out," I breathed as I retreated from the room and made my way back to the second floor. My footsteps sounded like thunder claps as I moved down the corridor to the room. My fingers shook as I reached for the doorknob. I was surprised I didn't jiggle the thing out of the door when I turned it.

Get it together, Darcy.

The room was in somewhat less disarray than my last visit. The bridesmaids' dresses had now been removed entirely, collected as evidence I suspected. The cases had been closed and pushed off to one side and the beds had been made. I had no idea where to look. I still hadn't determined which case belonged to which woman.

"Guess I search them all," I muttered and got to work.

I rummaged through the first case and came up empty. The second case yielded only a pair of broken earrings and a dried out mascara brush buried beneath clothes. That left the simple black case propped up under the window. My stomach did a flip as I approached it. I eased it down flat and unzipped the top. The contents were neatly folded and organized, with shirts and undergarments in the top half and pants with shoes in the bottom. There wasn't much space to hide anything, but I still slid my hand around the edge of the interior, hoping to happen upon an unseen zipper compartment. Nothing.

I had no way of knowing when that conversation I'd glimpsed occurred. For all I knew Elise had gone back to wearing the necklace. Or she'd ignored her mother's directive entirely. But there was one last place I hadn't searched.

Casey's belongings.

I backed out of the room and crossed the hall to the partially open door leading to the room Casey had inhabited since Thursday night. She would have shared it on her wedding night with Andrew before heading off on their honeymoon.

Her wedding gown hung from the top of the closet door; its lacy train artfully gathered up at the bottom to keep it from getting dirty. I spotted a large garment bag and for a moment I wondered why she hadn't stowed it back in there. It didn't matter though. I needed to find the necklace. I could have used a plant-induced vision of Elise stashing it somewhere. When I reached out with my magic, I got nothing, not even a hazy vision of Casey's distraught sobs that had filled the house for days.

I rummaged through her suitcase and found extra makeup and hair pins along with the dress she'd worn to the rehearsal dinner. No necklace.

"Looking for this?" Elise's voice cut through the silence of the room and I whirled to face the still-open doorway, where the maid of honor now stood, holding the diamond necklace aloft in one hand.

"I would have thought getting drugged would have been enough to kill your curiosity."

"I'm resilient," I quipped, my palms growing sweaty again. "You knew what your mum did, didn't you? To Andrew."

Elise let out a bark of harsh laughter. "You've got it all wrong. She didn't kill him. I did."

19

———————

"*Y*ou?" But I'd seen her in the room with the other bridesmaids when Vinnie had gone to notify Casey of the death.

"What, you don't think I had it in me?"

"But they just wanted to scare him."

"They were still blinded by his charms. I knew he'd never stop hurting people, using them."

"So, you killed your own father?'

"He was no father to me. A glorified sperm donor at best."

Before I could ask any more questions the window behind me flew open with a chilling gust of air. The sensation of it on my skin matched what I'd felt before being drugged, but the intensity had gone up to ten. The click-clack of high heels on wood announced Catrina's presence as she came into view.

"Why don't we take this outside? I'd hate to ruin the house."

She gave a dismissive wave and my feet were off the ground in a matter of seconds. I flew backwards out the window and slammed hard into the ground. The air left my lungs with such force I thought I'd never breathe again. The world above me blinked out of focus as the jolt to my body caught up with my brain sending pain signals through me. Every part of me ached as I struggled to sit up. Tania and Maggie were nowhere to be seen. Had Catrina and Elise taken care of them while I snooped upstairs?

I managed to get to my feet just as Elise appeared on the grass in front of me. For a moment, her outline blurred. She reached a hand out and grabbed a fistful of my shirt, flinging me toward the fence. I landed with another painful 'oomph.'

"You saw the version of him he wanted you see," Elise continued. "I understood who he really was. A man who used people to get what he wanted."

"He never even knew you existed," I coughed, trying to get to my feet again.

"How would you know?'

"Because I saw your birth certificate. Your mum never listed a father."

"That doesn't matter. I watched him for months with Casey, the way he reeled her in. He didn't care about her or want to support her. He just wanted a younger woman on his arm … to make his rich friends jealous."

"If that's how you felt, why not tell Casey the truth and warn her off him that way?"

Elise's anger ebbed momentarily. "She wouldn't have believed me. It was easier to just go along with the plan."

"So, your plan was to ruin what was supposed to be the happiest day of her life? Doesn't seem like very good friend behavior. Definitely not maid of honor worthy. But then I bet you wormed your way in to make sure you'd be given that role."

"I knew she didn't really want to do it. So, it was easy to get her to agree to let me handle everything."

"And then you found his ex-wives and they fit perfectly into your plan to ruin things, didn't they?"

"Like I said, they were still swayed by his charms when I met them. Oh, sure, they hated him, too. But it was buried by time. They'd tried to move on with their lives. That's when I realized I had the perfect way to get back at him."

"How's that?"

"You wouldn't understand."

I finally managed to find my balance and stand up again. The grass beneath my feet might have been fading as winter approached, but it was still alive and I could feel it tickling the back of my mind, begging to help. I suspected she didn't realize yet that I, too, had magic like her and her mother. Time for a little display of my own power.

"I think you'll find I do," I quipped and spread my fingers out.

Directly beneath my hands in my shadow the grass rippled, growing visibly greener and more alive. It swayed and waved as the tiny shoots that had been stubby and brown moments ago, rose up to waist height.

"Nice trick," Elise scoffed, her voice coming from the side of the house.

I turned to see her and her mother striding toward me. I looked back to see her still standing in the yard with me, too. As the Elise in the side yard grew closer, the one who'd been explaining all of her machinations grew fuzzy around the edges. Finally, the two versions of Elise merged into one person. I blinked, the double exposure effect still wreaking havoc on my retinas. It finally made sense how someone had been able to move around without being seen.

"That's how you did it. You can astral project," I said, failing to keep the awe out of my voice.

"Do you want a gold star for figuring that out?" Elise sneered.

I turned my attention to Catrina. "Did you want him dead, too?"

"Andrew never truly understood the effect he had on people. Believe me, the world's better off without him in it."

"Then why lie to the others, make them think they were just going to scare him?"

"After me, I think Andrew realized he needed to find mundane women to snare with his charms. Less chance they'd be able to fight back. And honestly, they weren't that bright," Catrina answered.

Courtney had been smart enough to turn herself in and cooperate with the police. At least she'd get a reduced sentence. I suspected given time Colleen and Clara would throw their lots in with her.

Across the yard, Catrina held up her hand and a swirl of wind materialized, creating a mini cyclone between us. "You really should have stopped meddling in other people's business."

Letting Maggie fall under suspicion, however brief, made it my business. "I should have known it was you who tried to drug me," I said. "But how did you know I was even there?"

Catrina held up a phone with a different case from the one I'd discovered in the side table in her room. "You didn't think I would leave my daughter in there with dangerous chemicals unsupervised, did you?" She hit play on a video that showed me rummaging through the room and uncovering the flowers.

The one time Sam had actually respected someone's personal boundaries. "All three of the bouquets were dosed. The police told me as much."

"You weren't supposed to find him when you did," Elise explained unhelpfully.

"You were going to all be knocked out, so how could you have possibly done it. And if anyone else asked questions, you could blame it on the florist. The police would figure out her connection to Andrew and blame the jilted lover. Same with Clara and the food. Did she really remove the food or did you do that, too?"

"I'll never tell."

"Well, you didn't count on there being witnesses to your little meeting with Colleen at the rehearsal dinner," I commented.

"Guess I'd better tie up those loose ends," Elise taunted.

They'd clearly planned this for some time and weren't above letting other people take the fall for their crimes. My ears strained to hear police sirens in the distance. Surely Tania and Maggie had filled Chief Hayes in by now and he'd be swooping in for an arrest.. There was only silence beyond where we stood.

There was still one piece I was missing. "I don't understand the necklaces. You said Andrew's other exes were mundane. So why bother purchasing magical amulets?"

"They didn't need to have magic. I just needed them to channel all that anger and hate into the gems," Elise said. "And it was easy once I'd convinced them to take on Casey as a client. I was there for every meeting, facilitating everything for her as a good maid of honor."

"But wouldn't Andrew have noticed his exes running around behind the scenes, even if he wasn't that involved in planning?"

Elise gave a smirk. "The necklaces were spelled so he'd be compelled to look away and not pay attention to them."

"Why bother having them channel anything into it if you were just going to strangle him?'

"Because he needed to feel what they felt. He needed to know what he'd done to them. I let it all out, hit him with it as I squeezed the pathetic life out of him," Elise spat.

"Elise, shut up," Catrina huffed before sending the cyclone flying in my direction.

I threw my hands up to shield myself from the

oncoming torrent of wind. The sound of foliage cracking and bending against strong winds filled my ears. The grass I'd grown as a show of my power had formed a latticework, a wall of stiff grass and root. The tree that sat in the back corner of the yard had extended its barren branches to shield me, too. The wind battered the plants, but they didn't buckle or yield. The longer I held them though, the more my body felt the strain of channeling my magic after the fall out the window. My muscles ached as if I'd been running full speed and my joints throbbed.

I should have anticipated Elise's attack, but her astral form caught me off guard. I felt her hands wrap around my throat from behind and squeeze. Had this been how she'd managed to catch Andrew off guard, too? It could explain the gash on his cheek. If he'd truly gone to the bathroom looking for water to help his father, she could have been watching him unseen and slipped into the tiny room behind him.

I clawed at her hands, trying to loosen her grip on me, but it only fueled her anger. She dug her nails into the soft flesh of my throat and I could smell the copper in my blood as it stained her perfectly manicured nails. My vision grew spotty as oxygen fought to get to my brain and my body tried to get air into my lungs. I did the only thing I could do. I jabbed my right elbow straight back, colliding painfully with her sternum. It sent shockwaves down my arm, but it was enough to force her to loosen her grip.

I staggered forward as Catrina's whirlwind died down. The grasses remained firm as a barrier between us, but what I really needed was one between Elise's astral form and me.

I turned to look at the projection. "You made one mistake," I coughed.

"What's that?"

"The flowers. I don't know how, but you managed to leave a petal behind."

"So, what? It could have come from any number of places."

I heard a car engine rumble somewhere nearby as both Elises began circling me, edging around the foliage barrier I'd erected. Out of the corner of my eye, I caught Catrina waving her fingers at the ground. I didn't realize what she was doing until large clods of dirt flew into the air, taking pieces of the latticework grass with it. I couldn't focus on all of this at once, so I turned my attention back to Elise.

"You're right. It could have come from anywhere and if it had just been the police investigating, they probably would have just brushed it off as unimportant. But not me, plants are my specialty. They love to tell me things, show me where they belong. And that petal brought me to Dina's bouquet. I give you credit for handling her flowers. I'd say it was another bit of misdirection on your part, but you didn't even notice, did you?"

"No one's going to believe you. You don't have any proof," Elise's astral self taunted.

"I do." Casey's voice cut through the conversation like a machete.

We all turned to see the former bride standing in the yard, tear tracks marring her flushed cheeks. I saw Chief Hayes behind her with weapon drawn, but held lowered at his side. At least he wasn't charging in where he might accidentally hit me. Knowing the police chief wasn't in the mood to shoot me was a good sign.

"You don't know what you're talking about, Case," Elise said, her astral form disappearing.

"I heard what you said. I heard it all," Casey shouted, her hands balling into fists.

How had she known to come back? By the fact that all of the rooms were empty, I'd assumed Maggie had managed to corral her and the other women out of the house. But Maggie and Tania were also missing in action. Had they gone to the police with what we suspected?

"I did you a favor. I did us all a favor," Elise spat

back. "He would have ruined your life. And mine, because I would have had to pick up the pieces."

"Stop talking," Catrina snarled at her daughter, her hand clenching into a tight fist.

Elise's mouth clamped shut and her eyes widened as her mother literally forced her into silence. Casey closed the distance between her and Elise, and she raised a hand, ready to strike the woman who had pretended to have her back.

"I hate you!" Casey shouted and landed a solid blow to Elise's jaw.

That was enough for Chief Hayes and Vinnie to rush forward, weapons now raised and leveled at Elise and her mother. Vinnie skillfully pushed Casey away from the fray as he produced a pair of hand-cuffs and spun Elise around, tightening them around her wrists.

I didn't pay attention as the two women were read their rights and hauled off into a waiting police cruiser. Casey sunk to the grass, burying her head in her hands as the whole situation likely hit her like a ton of bricks.

My own ordeal hit me at the same moment and my body turned to jelly. My bones melted and I collapsed to the grass. At least I felt the soft carpeting of green cushion me this time.

I blinked my eyes closed for what felt like hours,

but couldn't have been more than a few minutes given Casey's proximity to me on the ground to find Tania and Maggie sitting beside me. Maggie pulled me into her lap and I tried not to wince as all the aches I'd felt from the fall renewed their discomfort.

"Ow," I moaned.

"What hurts?" Maggie's voice was gentle.

"Everything. Catrina threw me out a bloody second floor window."

"*Dios mio*," Tania whispered. "How did you manage not to break anything?"

I patted the small patch of vibrant green grass beneath me. It hadn't felt like it broke my fall, but it must have been just enough to keep me from breaking any bones. "All that practice came in handy. And look, I caught the killers."

"I should have realized magic was involved." Maggie continued to cradle me in her lap.

"I think whatever floral scent I had picked up on was a sign of her magic. Somehow she left that behind. I don't even think she knew about it. The flower petal was a mistake."

"And it was the one clue you couldn't let go of," Tania said.

I never would have thought a single flower petal would have been enough to crack an entire murder case. And yet, once again, my connection to the natural world around us had led to bringing closure to another grieving family. As I finally managed to stand with Maggie's help, I caught sight of Chief Hayes standing in the driveway. And I could almost swear he gave me a smile.

20

It had taken me longer to recover from my confrontation with Elise and Catrina than I'd hoped. At least I didn't need to make a second visit to the hospital. Maggie had been kind enough to lend her healing magic to keep me comfortable as I convalesced.

The town had finally settled down from the drama as Thanksgiving hit. It being my first time celebrating the holiday, I simply went along with whatever those around me were doing. That meant helping Tania brine an enormous ten-pound turkey. I reminded her that I wasn't the world's biggest fan of the bird. Since it was back to just the two of us in the B&B, there was no need for her to cook so much food.

My concerns didn't dissuade her from cooking

the bird along with a host of other sides and fixings like mashed potatoes, creamed corn, sweet potato casserole, and biscuits. And then there were the pies.

"Are you absolutely sure we need five different kinds of pies?" I protested the morning of Thanksgiving as she stood in the kitchen rolling out pie crusts into a row of pans.

"This is your first Thanksgiving with us, you'll learn that this is exactly the right amount of food," Tania answered.

"Yeah, but you've made enough food for a small army. While I know I need to keep working my way back up to full strength I'm pretty sure all of this food is just going to make me sleepy."

She waved me off. "Go get some rest. Dinner will be at two."

"Who eats dinner at bloody two in the afternoon?" I grumbled.

"Oh, you get to experience the joy that is American football," Sam crooned as I marched upstairs to my room.

"No thanks. Sports aren't really my thing."

"You mean you don't love watching grown men headbutt each other for money?" Sam laughed.

"I'll pass. I've had enough head-numbing violence for a while, thanks."

"I should have warned you," Sam said, floating behind me into my room.

"Warned me about what?"

"The crazy lady and her nutso daughter."

"You had no way of knowing what they'd planned," I reminded him.

"Maybe not, but I knew something was off about them. I should have said something before, but I'm pretty sure they both saw me."

It made sense in hindsight. Sam could only be seen by people with magic. The two women had both been witches, so of course they would have been able to see Sam.

"I was keeping an eye on the mother like you told me to the day you were attacked ... and I should have felt the magic."

"I don't blame you, Sam. So, you better stop blaming yourself. Besides, it all worked out in the end."

"I just would have hated for something to happen to you," he admitted.

"You care. I'm touched."

"You make the afterlife interesting," he said.

"Happy to be entertainment I guess. But right now I need to get some rest. Healer's orders."

Sam gave me a wry grin. "Wouldn't want to upset the woman who holds ... everything in her hands."

"Sod off."

I snuggled beneath the blankets and closed my eyes. Thankfully, sleep came quickly and the dreams about finding Andrew's body had faded. With all of the women involved in his murder behind bars, those left in their aftermath could begin to piece their lives back together. And Brookhaven could get back to its usual routine.

When I woke, I could hear voices in the hall. I sat up, my hair falling into my face, obstructing my vision as I tried to make out who was here. I scrambled for my phone on the bedside table and realized it was already one o'clock. Tania's proclamation that dinner would be served at two spurred me to my feet. I staggered out of bed and into the hall just in time to find Maggie and Tania both standing there.

"How are you feeling?" Maggie took a step closer to me.

"Better. Thanks for everything you've been doing."

"My pleasure."

Behind her, Sam materialized long enough to make a lewd gesture or two before disappearing again. "So, did you just come by to check up on me?"

"Tania invited me for dinner. I didn't have any other plans, so figured why not spend it with my friends."

"The rest of the guests will be here in about forty-five minutes."

"Other guests?"

Tania just nodded and spun on her heel, heading back down to the kitchen. The scents of all of the food she'd prepared wafted up the stairs and made my mouth water. Even the turkey.

"Uh, not to be a bad host or anything, but do you mind if I hop in the shower?"

"Not at all. I'll just see what Tania needs help with."

"Careful, she might enlist you," I called with a laugh before heading back to my room for a change of clothes.

When I emerged twenty minutes later, I felt human and the most normal I'd been in days. I swept my hair into a messy knot on the top of my head as I descended the stairs. I was halfway down when I heard a knock at the door. Tania had said our dinner companions wouldn't be arriving for another twenty-five minutes.

"I'll get it," I called and raced to the door. Ginny stood on the doorstep with a bottle of wine and a covered basket. "Uh, what are you doing here?"

"I felt bad turning down Tania's invite for dinner. I've got other plans, but I thought I'd bring by some dessert and some wine."

"Did she invite the whole town?" I blurted.

"No. And don't worry, she invites me every year. It's kind of a running joke at this point. She invites me, and I always say no, but bring over a little something."

"Well, we've got a mountain of food and enough pies to float a cruise ship, but thanks. I'm sure this is going to be brilliant."

"I'm glad you figured out what happened."

"Not sure your brother agrees."

"He won't admit it to anyone else, but I know he was grateful for the help. Magic makes him a little touchy. So, thank you for getting the truth to come out."

"Well, uh, you're welcome."

"Happy Thanksgiving, Darcy."

"Same to you, Ginny."

She turned on her heel and headed down the porch steps out of view. I had just enough time to carry the basket and wine into the kitchen. Presented them to Tania, who laughed and smiled, before another knock resounded on the front door.

"That should be the rest of our dinner party," Tania called as she stirred a pot of thick gravy.

I marched back through the front hall and opened the door to find Gerry and Casey standing there, side by side. We all stood staring awkwardly at each other for a few moments before I regained my composure.

"Hi. Come on in. Here, let me take your coats."

I accepted the overcoat Gerry slipped off and the knee-length coat Casey held out. She wouldn't meet my gaze as I hung their coats and followed them through the kitchen where Tania stood still manning the stove. Maggie had found a bottle opener and was already opening the bottle of wine from Ginny.

"Can I help with something?" Gerry asked.

"You're our guest, Gerry. You can help by sitting down and letting me bring you food," Tania replied with a shooing motion.

"Come on, you can help me bring in the side dishes," Maggie stage whispered.

Gerry accepted the butter dish and basket of biscuits while Maggie carried in the corn and the casserole. I followed after them with the mashed potatoes and jam for the biscuits.

"We'll carve the turkey in here and bring it out for people to pick their choice of meat on that serving dish," Tania instructed, gesturing to a large silver platter and accompanying serving fork.

Casey stood there looking shellshocked as Tania

moved around her like a ballet dancer executing languid moves. I gently put a hand on Casey's elbow, ushered her into the dining room, and into an empty chair.

"Wine?" I offered, but she shook her head.

In short order, Tania appeared with the turkey piled high on the serving platter and set it into the middle of the table. Even with just the five of us, I questioned the amount of food she'd prepared.

"Thank you all for being here with us today. We may not be related by blood, but we are bound by circumstance and by friendship," Tania said with her head bowed. "Now, please eat."

Silence descended on our small group, save for the occasional clank of cutlery on dinnerware or the scraping of the bottom of a serving dish. I shouldn't have questioned Tania's culinary estimation. By the time we'd finished the main course, there were only scraps left.

"I'm too full for pie," I announced, pushing my plate away.

"Don't worry, you won't be when it's time for dessert," Tania said.

She directed us to the living room where we spread out across the space. Maggie sat near Gerry and Tania retreated briefly to the kitchen. I heard the telltale sound of water in the sink as she rinsed dishes. I settled on the couch beside Casey.

"I'm surprised to see you back in town," I said.

"Gerry invited me. And I didn't have anyone else to spend the holiday with."

"I'm sorry. What about your friends? Isn't friends-giving a thing?"

"Dina went home to her parents in California, but I don't have the money to cover a flight. I spent most of it on the wedding." Tears sparkled in her eyes at the mention of her failed nuptials.

"Well, I'm glad you found somewhere you felt comfortable coming for the holiday."

"I almost didn't come." For the first time since arriving, she met my gaze. "But then Gerry told me you'd be here, too, and I realized I had to come."

"Because I was going to be here?"

She nodded. "After everything that happened with Elise and her mom, I didn't get the chance to say thank you."

"I didn't really do anything," I said, trying to brush off her appreciation.

"You helped a complete stranger get closure and you made me realize the darkness I'd let into my life. I owe you for that."

"Please, you don't owe me anything. I was just trying to figure out what happened. And things got a tad out of hand there at the end. But everything's been set as right as it can be. If I could wave a magic wand and take it all away, I'd have done it."

"Magic is real. I know that now. And I understand that to some extent the feelings I had for Andrew were because of his magic. But I wouldn't want you to erase it all. I wouldn't have known what Elise had done if it weren't for you."

"I don't see how you can be so positive about the whole thing. Any of those women could have told you what you were walking into and they didn't. Maybe if they had, he'd still be alive," I said.

"You're right. But I also can see now why Elise was trying to keep me away from him. She knew who he was. But if she'd just told me that up front, I wouldn't have gotten involved. I would have respected what she was trying to tell me."

"Sorry to say, I think even if that were the case, he would have found someone else," Gerry interjected from across the room.

Both Casey and I turned our attention to the man sitting beside Maggie. He gripped the stem of his wine glass tight in both hands as he leaned forward.

"He was always close with his mother and I think in some ways, her magic affected him more than either of us realized. He craved that influence and that affection. I think perhaps he was trying to find something like that again in a prospective spouse. He thought maybe he'd found it with Catrina, but I don't think any of us realized she had magic of her own. Whether that cancelled his out, I couldn't say. But he ran through the next three, still never finding what he was looking for."

"You think he would have just gone on to find some other unsuspecting woman if I'd turned him down?" Casey reiterated.

"I do." His hands shook and I feared for the wine glass. Maggie apparently shared my concern, because she plucked it from his hands and set it on a side table. "I don't think he was ever going to fill that void left by his mother's passing. I'd hoped maybe it would be different with you, my dear. You were so vibrant, so kind, I'd hoped you would be what he needed."

"Turns out what he needed no one could give him," Casey said softly.

"You are going to come through this and you're going to find a way to move forward with your life," I said, trying to buck her up.

"A week or two ago I would have said you were full of it. But now, I think maybe you're right. I'm clearer headed than I've been in a long time and I see now that I wasn't meant to marry a man twice my age, even if he seemed like the perfect guy for me at the time. I'm not really ready to be married yet. I could have done without the traumatic way the universe taught me that particular lesson, but I see it now."

I looked to Gerry. "What about you? How are you holding up?"

"Oh, I'm going to be all right. I know I have people I can turn to if I need them," he admitted and looked toward the kitchen, "and I have to believe now that Andrew is finally at peace."

On that note, Tania appeared in the entryway to the dining room. Her face took on a temporarily pinched expression—no doubt she was picking up on the fraught emotions in the room. She relaxed a moment later. "I am sorry to interrupt a very important and what sounds like a very healing discussion, but would anyone like some dessert?"

I'd been so focused on the conversation; I hadn't even noticed the time passing. And when I thought about the half dozen pies waiting to be eaten in the other room, my stomach rumbled as if I hadn't eaten in days.

"Pie sounds nice," Casey said and stood, leading the procession back to the dining room.

I fell into step beside Maggie. "I am telling you;

Tania's got some extra hearth magic and she's been holding out on us."

"Or more likely you were just distracted by the conversation and forgot how full you were," Maggie replied.

"Nope, I'm sticking with the hearth magic theory. Prove me wrong."

Maggie just laughed and I slid into the seat beside her. She grabbed my hand under the table and gave it a light squeeze. "So, you still owe me a first date," she whispered as Tania passed around the dessert plates.

"I guess I do," I said.

"Don't worry, I know things are going to be hectic with the holidays coming up. How about we make an early New Year's Resolution to have that date before Valentine's Day?"

Warmth flooded every part of my body as I looked at her. It wasn't magic. Not in the sense of the supernatural abilities we shared. But it was a feeling I only associated with Maggie. It was safe, and loving ... and all mine.

As I took in the scene before me—pies circulating amongst smiling faces, I couldn't help but feel grateful for the family I'd found here in Brookhaven. I'd set out seeking a place in the world. It had grabbed me by the hand and pulled me straight here to these people. I couldn't have gotten through the last few weeks without Tania and Maggie, and couldn't quite put into words how important they'd become to me in such a few short months. I knew that whatever else lay ahead in the future, I could rely on them to get me through.

And I was grateful for the magic that continued to flourish and grow within me. I was finally starting to feel like I was becoming the person I was always meant to be. Winter might be on the way now, but I couldn't wait to see what came when spring bloomed anew.

QUICK AUTHOR'S NOTE

Since Darcy solved the two cases I'd set out for her in the first two books, I knew book 3 was going to be an unrelated case. For careful readers, it was foreshadowed in book two. I enjoyed getting to let Darcy and Maggie have more of a team-up in this one, especially as Maggie was the one in potential jeopardy this time.

I loved getting to see the beginnings of their romance. I knew some people would likely expect her to end up with Chief Hayes but I wanted to be different and I just adore Maggie and Darcy together. We need more strong representation in this genre!

I have to admit, this book was a breeze to write and I'm not sure why. It just flowed easily without too many snags. I loved that the killer wasn't obvious and their motives weren't entirely typical. I also thought it was about time Darcy faced off against an actual magically-inclined killer!

So what lays ahead for Darcy and company as we move into book 4? Well, family was quite important in *High Fidelity* and that continues to be the case in *High Hopes*. Let's just say some of Darcy's questions about where her magic came from might finally get some answers.

Turn the page for a sneak peek at High Hopes...

HIGH HOPES

Montagues, Magic and Murder!

Life in Brookhaven has settled down for Darcy. She's gained more control over and confidence in her magic. And she's happily dating Maggie. When she discovers she has family in the area, Darcy can't imagine things going any better.

But when a night out at the theater for her cousin's production of Romeo and Juliet turns deadly and Darcy's new cousin looks like a prime suspect, she's bound up in another murder investigation.

Proving her family's innocence seems simple enough but the more Darcy digs, the more she unearths a twisted obsession and dangerous magic. Will the trap she lays for the killer force a confessions, or will they slip away, leaving only tragedy in their wake?

Scan the QR code to buy High Hopes today

ABOUT THE AUTHOR

S.E. Biglow is the pen name of *USA Today* bestselling author Sarah Biglow. She lives in Massachusetts with her husband and son. She is a licensed attorney and spends her days combatting employment discrimination as an Investigator with the Massachusetts Commission Against Discrimination.

You can find an up-to-date list of all my books here

www.ingramcontent.com/pod-product-compliance
Lightning Source LLC
Chambersburg PA
CBHW051306210726
48287CB00002B/696